SKYLAR

SKYLAR

A STORY BY **MARY CUFFE-PEREZ**

ILLUSTRATED BY
RENATA LIWSKA

PHILOMEL BOOKS

PHILOMEL BOOKS
A division of Penguin Young Readers Group.
Published by The Penguin Group.
Penguin Group (USA) Inc., 375 Hudson Street, New York, NY 10014, U.S.A.
Penguin Group (Canada), 90 Eglinton Avenue East, Suite 700, Toronto,
Ontario M4P 2Y3, Canada (a division of Pearson Penguin Canada Inc.).
Penguin Books Ltd, 80 Strand, London WC2R 0RL, England.
Penguin Ireland, 25 St. Stephen's Green, Dublin 2, Ireland
(a division of Penguin Books Ltd).
Penguin Group (Australia), 250 Camberwell Road, Camberwell,
Victoria 3124, Australia (a division of Pearson Australia Group Pty Ltd).
Penguin Books India Pvt Ltd, 11 Community Centre,
Panchsheel Park, New Delhi - 110 017, India.
Penguin Group (NZ), 67 Apollo Drive, Rosedale, North Shore 0632,
New Zealand (a division of Pearson New Zealand Ltd).
Penguin Books (South Africa) (Pty) Ltd, 24 Sturdee Avenue,
Rosebank, Johannesburg 2196, South Africa.
Penguin Books Ltd, Registered Offices: 80 Strand,
London WC2R 0RL, England.

Published simultaneously in Canada. Printed in the United States of America.
Design by Marikka Tamura.
Library of Congress Cataloging-in-Publication Data
Cuffe-Perez, Mary, 1946–
Skylar / Mary Cuffe-Perez; illustrated by Renata Liwska.
p. cm.
Summary: Skylar, who claims he was once wild, leads four pond geese in their first attempt
at migration when an injured heron asks their help in reaching Lost Pond, where the annual
Before the Migration Convention is about to be held.
[1. Canada Goose—Fiction. 2. Geese—Fiction. 3. Birds—Migration—Fiction.]
I. Liwska, Renata, ill. II. Title. PZ7.C8927Sky 2008 [Fic]—dc22 2007020437
ISBN 978-0-399-24543-5
10 9 8 7 6 5 4 3 2 1

To my husband, Ken,
for his belief in *Skylar*, and in me.

CHAPTER 1
GOOSE HILL

They're coming," gasped the woman, dropping the handles of the wheelbarrow.

"Who?" asked the child, swinging around in all directions. The woman did not answer. She was already rushing into the house. The little girl dropped the load of wood she was carrying and followed.

"Who?" she asked again from the doorway, though by now she knew and was only asking for the fun of it. She pressed her hands over her mouth, pushing back a tickle of laughter. Her great-grandmother was on a collision course with everything in the kitchen, mumbling to herself and opening and closing cupboard drawers, closet doors, knocking over the broom, startling the cat, then finally, with a gush of relief, snatching her binoculars from the windowsill. She rushed past the child, out the door, throwing back the answer just before the question was asked again:

"The geese!"

With a loud whoop of joy, the girl grabbed the notebook with the stubby pencil stuck in its spiral binding that was always kept on the kitchen windowsill beside the binoculars. Holding the notebook above her head, she ran past her great-grandmother. She laughed herself nearly out of breath as she bolted through the waist-high field grass to the little rise in back of the house. The yelping of the geese was closer now, though the flock had not broken into view.

The woman stopped midway up the hill to catch her breath. When she was younger, there had been plenty of time—between the first sounding of the geese to the sighting of them—to reach the top of the hill. Now there was not quite enough time. The woman glowed inside at the sight of the child, already there. A small, dark, agitated figure under the sugar maple that had lost its leaves top down. Waving the notebook, the child jumped up and down in the fallen leaves, urging her great-grandmother along and pointing toward the northeastern horizon.

"I'm coming," the woman called back.

Many years ago, when she had first moved into the farmhouse, when it was surrounded by fields and forest and there was not another house to be seen, the woman had named this little rise Goose Hill. From the top of the rise, under the maple, she had watched countless seasons pass with the spring and fall migrations of songbirds, raptors, ducks and geese. She had come here with her own children, then with her grandchildren and now with her great-grandchild, whose hand she reached out for now as she climbed the last few feet to the top of the hill.

"There! There!" the girl shouted as the woman braced herself against the trunk of the maple to scan the northeastern horizon where the child was pointing. Her hands trembled as she swung her binoculars along the faint green light where sky met the black, peaked tree line. Then she saw them. Exploding out of the horizon, tearing everything earthbound loose—trees, hills, darkness, herself. As always, she felt herself pulled with them.

"One, two, three . . . ," the child counted as the geese swelled above them in a rollicking joyous noise, their black necks outstretched, underbellies gleaming and wing tips flashing as they dipped into the day's last light. They passed overhead in two broken lines that parted, seemed to disconnect, then drifted back together.

The woman was sure she heard the whistle of the wind through their flight feathers but knew this could not be. The geese were almost two thousand feet above them.

"Eighteen," the girl called as the geese thundered past, now aligned in an almost perfect V formation. The girl wrote the number carefully in the notebook.

"How many now?"

"One hundred and fifty-three," the girl announced after frowning over the figures in the notebook for some time.

"Those will be the last this year," sighed the woman.

Within minutes, the geese had vanished behind the line of hills to the south, their honking calls clattering behind them.

"Gone," the girl announced, dropping the word into the well of silence.

It was never so still as when the geese had passed.

When the woman reached to take her hand, the girl was already running down the hill toward the house. At the bottom of the hill, she stopped abruptly and turned to peer back up the hill.

"Gram . . . ?" she called uncertainly. "Where are you?"

"I'm here," answered the woman, making her way, carefully now, down the hill.

The little rise from where the two stood to watch the migrating geese was a drumlin, made by glaciers many thousands of years ago, a landmark locked in the memories of the geese as they passed over it. To geese, all things are landmarks to be locked in their memories, even the old woman who came to the same spot on the hill year after year.

The flock that passed over the drumlin where the woman and child stood was composed of three families of Canada geese. It was the sixth migration for the strong gander at the point of the flock. For the juvenile geese that took up the rear, it was the first. The younger geese hardly looked down at the land below them. They were just learning to fly in formation, and all their attention was trained on the older geese ahead and the steady stream of instructions they honked back to the juveniles: lift higher, angle to the right, drop back, keep up.

The next landmark was the highway that stretched below like a black frozen river. The highway cut between two ridges, also the work of glaciers many thousands of years before there were any roads at all—a time locked in the memories of the geese, when there was less to remember, just the natural swell and bloom of the earth below. Now there were frequent, often confusing landmarks. Many of them, like the highway and the pond that came next, made by humans.

Geese never fail to memorize bodies of water, no matter how small. But this pond was nothing more than a blink in their memories. They would never seek refuge in such a pond. Everything about it was suspicious. Except for a few cattails at one end, nothing grew around the edges. Instead, curious animal forms were posed around it, all frozen in unnatural positions. Even the five geese clustered on its shores seemed artificial, though they flapped their wings and stretched their necks like live geese. And one of these geese would always extend a contact call as the geese passed, but the wild geese never answered. This year, as they had always done, the flock blinked once, marked the pond and its strange inhabitants in their memories and flew on.

CHAPTER 2
THE WHO-ON

One morning in early November, five geese awoke to find a great blue heron on the opposite shore of their pond. The geese did not know it was a great blue heron at first. The bird stood so perfectly still the geese were not sure if it was real at all. It could have been another statue. The pond was encircled by wading birds, frogs, toadstools and gnomes, all placed there by the people who lived in the big white house with columns that overlooked the pond.

"Oh, no," whispered Weedle, the smallest goose. His round black eyes darted from the two frozen figures of flamingos at one end of the pond to the heron at the other. "Not another one of *them*."

The group of geese leaned in the direction of the strange animal at the other end of the pond. It made a striking figure against the lavender sky. "It looks very wild, whatever it is," whispered Weedle. The pond itself seemed wild with the heron there, though the pond, like the statues that surrounded it, had been made by the people who lived in the white house with columns. The pond, the geese and the house were all within a suburban neighborhood near a large city in upstate New York. But at that moment, as the geese all stretched their long necks toward the heron, nothing passed on the highway that ran in front of the pond; nothing seemed to move.

Then the heron tilted its head slightly and the geese clustered together in alarm. Except for Skylar, the largest goose. Skylar pulled himself up to look even taller than he was.

"What is it?" gasped Loomis, a long, lanky, pot-bellied goose. Loomis, just a few days older than Weedle, was twice as large. He had grown so fast none of his parts were well acquainted. He always seemed to be moving in many directions at once.

"A heron," came Skylar's loud honk of authority from behind them.

"A who-on?" asked Weedle.

"A heron, you moron," said Loomis, who did not know a heron from a sparrow or what he himself was. He jabbed Weedle sharply with his beak. The smaller goose lunged back, just as Roosevelt stepped between the two.

"Whatever it is," said Roosevelt, bouncing Weedle off his feet, "it's a long way from the zoo." Roosevelt was the oldest and fattest goose, and he always liked to have something to say on a subject.

Esther, a goose darker than the others, cocked her head at Roosevelt. "Herons live in the north, like we do. Until the ponds and lakes begin to freeze over. Then they migrate south. Like wild geese. This one must be migrating."

Skylar gave a goose grunt. He disliked this tendency of Esther's to be right. She seemed to know more things than a pond goose had any right to know, but even when Skylar talked over her, she always seemed to have the last word. Skylar did not like this at all, so he tried to ignore Esther, when it was possible to do so.

"Well," said Skylar with a shake of his tail feathers, "we could sit here all day listening to what *you* think. Or *I* could find out." Skylar puffed up his feathers, strode over to the pond and swam toward the heron. The other geese watched with interest. Loomis and Weedle, beaks still open, turned their attention from each other to see what would happen between Skylar and the heron.

"Skylar will find out what it is," said Weedle, who made a habit of studying Skylar's every move. "He used to be wild, too, you know." He looked eagerly from Roosevelt to Loomis, but the two geese ignored him. Their attention was drawn into Skylar's wake as he paddled toward a confrontation with the heron. "He can speak to wild things," Weedle finished quietly to himself.

The closer Skylar came to the tall, stately bird, the less confident he felt. He was aware of how his plump body listed from side to side as he paddled through the water. He saw how perfectly the heron fit just where it stood, among the cattails at the edge of the pond, against the sky and the distance. Skylar churned closer, under the remote gaze of the heron. He saw as the heron tilted his head to adjust to Skylar's level that he had only one eye, a piercing golden eye. The bird did not say anything.

"Look here," said Skylar as brusquely as he could manage, "you seem to be in the wrong pond."

Without a shade of expression in its golden eye, the heron replied, "I do?"

Skylar nodded his head gravely. "You're not the right sort at all for this pond."

The heron's gaze shifted over Skylar's head to the four geese gathered at the other end of the pond, their necks outstretched to catch the conversation between the two.

"This is our pond, you see," Roosevelt shouted from the other side of the pond, because he always liked to add something.

"This is not Lost Pond?" asked the heron.

"Lost Pond?" repeated Skylar loudly. "You thought *our* pond was Lost Pond? Lost Pond in the Adirondack Mountains?" Skylar turned to include the other geese in the joke. His confidence began to rise. "Hey, Roosevelt," he called, "does this look like the Adirondacks to you?" And he squawked his goose laugh until the others joined in, though they were not sure what they were laughing at. None of the geese, except Skylar, had ever been to the Adirondack Mountains. Those great, thrusting peaks and primitive forests were far to the north at the top of New York State, near Canada.

Feeling much taller now, Skylar turned back to the heron, who did not seem to understand the joke either. "Lost Pond is thousands of wing beats from here. How could you get so lost?"

"I must get to Lost Pond," said the heron, ignoring the question. "That's where the Before the Migration Convention is held each year. I must find it before five more sunsets. I'll be left behind unless I arrive at Lost Pond in time for the migration." The heron shifted from one leg to the other. "I can't be left behind," he said, with just a hint of anxiety.

"It is well known," said Skylar with a flap and quick adjustment of his wings, "that herons do not have a very refined sense of direction, like we geese. But I would think that even a heron . . . even a one-eyed heron . . . could find Lost Pond." Skylar swam in wide circles around the heron as he spoke. "Even I, who have not been a goose on the wing since I was a juvenile, could still find Lost Pond."

"Then you will take me there?" said the heron, lowering his head to catch Skylar's eye as he swam by.

Skylar stopped swimming. He bobbed like a decoy in the water. He could hear the others making little chuckling noises on the shore behind him.

"Yes, Skylar," said Roosevelt, "you can show the way." Now the geese were honking with laughter.

"You *are* the point goose," Loomis taunted. "Isn't that what you always call yourself?" His long, loose goose body began to lurch with laughter.

"Or are you a point goose without a point?" added Roosevelt. He thought this was so clever his honking laughter filled the November sky, causing the people in the houses surrounding the pond to look up at the sky for the sight of geese passing.

For several minutes, Loomis and Roosevelt kept up their honking. Esther had grown tired of the joke, and Weedle, who admired Skylar beyond all else, was having no part of it. He hunkered on the shore of the pond beside Esther and glared at Loomis and Roosevelt until their goose laughter shook down to a few *ker-honk*s and *ark*s. The heron tilted his head to one side. He did not understand these geese.

The heron could not know that Loomis and Roosevelt and even Esther had wanted a chance to laugh at Skylar for as long as they had all been in the pond together. They were tired of Skylar's soaring tales about his fabled migration, which had begun with a juvenile flight cut short by an ice storm and grew by many thousands of miles and experiences each time he told it. All they knew for sure was that they had never seen him fly any farther than from one end of the pond to the next. Mostly, he beat the air with his wings when he was bullying one of the other geese. Except for Weedle, none of the geese believed his stories anymore. All they knew for sure was that his story ended as theirs had. They were pond geese now.

Their laughter said all this: Skylar . . . claimed to be a point goose but was nothing more than a pond goose, living among statues of frogs and flamingos. Skylar . . . ate what was handed to him and knew no world wider than a man-made pond. Skylar . . . their laughter pelted him again and again until he rose up against it, his wings spread and his neck arched in fury. He half ran, half flew across the pond.

"I'll show the way all right," he hissed into the faces of the stunned geese, "and you fat four will be my flock!"

. . .

None of the geese slept that night, though Skylar, huddled into himself, pretended to. All night he thought about "the way" he had promised to lead the geese and the heron. He had told so many stories about his migration, he did not know what was story and what was real. In fact, he hardly remembered flying at all, only the storm that ended his first migration, the ice closing in on him and the vanishing calls of the other geese. How could he find the way if he could not even recall his own interrupted migration? Sometimes the memory of the way glowed so brightly inside him he was sure he could find it. Then it dissolved and he was not sure at all. He wondered if any of the other pond geese had ever seen the way. Perhaps Esther had, for she all too often chimed in with some unsettling piece of information she had no right knowing. Skylar stretched out his neck to catch the low, anxious conversation of the geese gathered on the opposite shore.

"He didn't mean it, of course," said Roosevelt. "After all, we are not wild geese. We have never really flown anywhere." Only Loomis nodded his head vaguely in agreement. Weedle looked confused.

Esther was gazing skyward. One by one, the geese followed her gaze. The half-moon was at its highest point in the sky and the distance was radiant with promise. Over the last few weeks, just like every year at this time, flock after flock of Canada geese had flown thousands of feet above them on their migration south. Their barking calls always stirred something in the pond geese, but they did not understand what it was or why it made them feel all at once sad, restless and left behind. This feeling did not leave them all during the months of October and November, even though each time the wild geese passed, Roosevelt would say something like, "Poor fools. Probably lost. What wouldn't they give for a pond like this, to be fed every day and never wanting . . . never wanting."

Still, not a single wild goose ever landed in their pond.

"We're the same as they are," Esther said, for she knew what the other geese were thinking.

Each of the geese had come to the pond from somewhere else. Skylar had been rescued as a fallen juvenile during his first migration. Loomis, Weedle and Roosevelt had been born in city parks, where they were captured as goslings. Then the geese were adopted by the people in the white house on the hill, who wanted geese to decorate and animate their pond. None of the geese knew where Esther had come from or why she knew so much. She was slightly smaller and darker than Skylar, Roosevelt and Loomis, but much larger than Weedle.

"We're not the same," said Loomis. "They're real geese. Wild geese."

"But we are geese . . . Canada geese . . . just like the geese that fly overhead."

"We are?" asked Weedle, looking down at himself as if he expected to find another body there. Weedle was not the same breed of Canada goose as the others. He was a cackling goose, only half the size of the giant Canada goose. His voice was distinctive, too—a piercing bark that had a tendency to veer wildly out of control when he became excited.

"Of course," replied Esther. "We look the same—more or less—don't we?" The geese, as if for the first time, studied one another closely. They were different sizes and shapes, and Esther was darker than the others, but they all had the distinctive markings of Canada geese—long, black necks and brindle feathers on their wings and backs.

They all had the same face marking—a white chin flap stretching from cheek to cheek. "We can call back to them in the same voice." She looked at Weedle. "More or less. We could even fly if we tried." Esther turned her gaze to the house on the hill above the pond. "We live in this place because we were brought here when we were very young. We never learned the wild ways. There are no dangers here."

"Dangers? What dangers?" asked Loomis, looking around the pond. Loomis, like the other geese, knew danger existed, for he heard it in the faraway thunder of guns each fall. But these distant sounds, like the passing of traffic, the barking of chained dogs, carried no immediate threat. They were no more alarming than the ceramic frogs and plastic flamingos that surrounded their pond.

"And there is no hunger to drive us," Esther continued. "We have grown fat on the grain they feed us and have never tried our wings. At least," she corrected, "not for a very, very long time."

"That's right," said Roosevelt. "There is no reason to leave. There is no good to come of it."

Esther gave a little dip of her head and snorted at Roosevelt. Then she turned back to the other geese. "There are many places beyond this pond," she said earnestly. She searched the skies again above her. The other geese could not help but look, too.

Esther was known among the geese as the "sky watcher," for no matter what she was doing or what was happening around her, her attention inevitably was drawn to the skies. She was always reading the weather fronts, and occasionally she would call to the passing flocks of wild geese.

"The world is large," Esther continued. The moon was nearly in back of them now and fading with the dawn. "I have heard this in the calling of the geese. I know you have heard it, too. There are other places. We could go there."

"Don't be ridiculous, Esther," said Roosevelt sternly. "The world is full of dangers, just as you said. We would be crazy to leave such a safe place. If Skylar was a wild goose, as he *claims*, he would know that a wild goose is a hunted goose. His pride is speaking, not his sense. We can never leave this pond!"

"Never leave this pond" seemed to hang in the air. It had an unsettling effect on the geese. The geese all secretly imagined that one day they would leave the pond behind. Instead of gazing longingly at what passed overhead, they would know the world from dazzling heights. They would fly among the wild geese. They all believed that someday, on just the right day, they would know the way. Since they did not know how to say this, they began to prod one another with wing slaps, with hisses and pecking. Finally, Weedle, who was getting the worst of it from Loomis, pulled himself free of the jostling and looked over at Skylar, a dark form on the other side of the pond.

"We can go as far as Lost Pond," Weedle said in a loud, determined voice. "Skylar can take us that far and back." Skylar's name shot several octaves higher than the other words and rattled into the distance.

CHAPTER 3
"WE'RE GONE!"

The sun opened the horizon like an invitation. A rich orange light bathed the geese lined up on the shore of the pond. Their excitement made it hard for them to stand at attention, which the situation demanded.

Skylar, looking like a plump, feathered general, marched up and down in front of his small flock, inspecting, nodding and making curious clucking sounds. The announcement had been made: Skylar would lead the heron to Lost Pond, and he expected the four pond geese, as his flock, to follow. Now he waited for the excuses, complaints, refusals, which he was sure would come. He stared hard at each goose as if he meant to find a weakness and expose it.

"If anyone chooses not to go, let me hear it now!" he barked, planting himself in front of the geese. There was no reply.

The four geese stood rigidly before him, as if a breath or twitch might betray their determination. None of them knew whether they could fly across the street, let alone to Lost Pond, but they knew they would follow Skylar.

This was not because they had faith in the arrogant goose who was their self-proclaimed leader. Only Weedle believed in him. And Skylar, for all his bluster, depended upon Weedle to believe in him—to nod in wide-eyed agreement at whatever he said even if he didn't understand, to watch and listen and follow him anywhere. None of the other geese, however, shared this devotion. Skylar's ego was too big for their small pond. They often jostled it among themselves with jokes and gossip as if it were some inflated toy. Still, in their artificial world, where most of the animals were ceramic or plastic, Skylar was as close to a flock leader as they would come.

After Skylar's announcement, the geese were uncharacteristically silent. All were aware, in some way, that this was the biggest moment of their lives.

They agreed, by way of their silence, to be Skylar's flock, even though it meant leaving their safe suburban pond for the perils of a world they knew very little about. One by one, they glided into the pond behind Skylar and swam over to address the heron—now known among them as the Who-on. The stately bird was still standing at the end of the pond where the cattails grew. It seemed as though the Who-on had not changed position all night.

"We have decided to rescue you," Skylar announced. "We will take you to Lost Pond." He waited for a response from the Who-on, but the big bird seemed intent on something in the water below. "But you must remember," continued Skylar, "to stay far in back of the flock. Thirty feet, no closer. It would be an embarrassment, you understand, to have a heron flying with a flock of geese."

The Who-on was busy swallowing a bullhead whole. He simply blinked his one eye at Skylar and gave no indication whether he understood or not.

"It is late to migrate," said Skylar, beginning to like the sound of his words, "but fortunately not too late. Geese frequently migrate well into

November in mild winters and occasionally winter here, too, but your . . . kind . . . aren't as hardy as geese and you are frequently"—he paused—"lost to the elements."

"Lost to the elements," repeated Weedle, sweeping his wings in the air.

Skylar ignored Weedle and addressed the horizon. The ring of authority in his own voice gave him courage. He spoke with assurance of landmarks, wind currents and the formation they would fly. It sounded real, and also wonderfully adventurous and flamboyant. Just the thought of using their wings to fly rather than to merely flap for the entertainment of the people in the house on the hill and to impress one another was thrilling to the geese.

Skylar's words did more than stir the imaginations of the geese. They flicked on the remembering light within each of them, and for that moment, each of them saw the way. The remembering light is shared by all geese. It illuminates the way. The way is one of five major migration routes that cross the globe, stretching from the North Pole to the South Pole. All wild geese have migrated along one of these five routes since before ancient peoples began to look into the sky and marvel at the "hounds of heaven" passing above them in great migratory waves. The way is drawn by the pattern of stars, the earth's magnetic field, the winds, the course of the sun, the contours of the earth. All geese are born with a remembering light of the way.

For geese, such as the pond geese, who have never migrated, the remembering light is very dim. It flares to the call of passing wild geese, but falters and dims once they have passed. The pond geese knew they could share this memory with the wild geese if only they had the courage or strength of wing to follow, or as Roosevelt was always saying, "if the people didn't feed us so much." But the time, it seemed, was never right. The time was not right now either. They were still five fat pond geese. Nevertheless, the time was here. The geese watched and listened to Skylar intently. The heron studied the water.

Using his whole body to demonstrate, Skylar gave a lengthy description of the formation. Weedle mirrored his every gesture. Since the flock was small, he said, they would fly in half of the typical V formation of a larger flock. They would form a wedge, he explained, lifting one wing, with himself in front to break up the wind currents and create an updraft. Roosevelt would follow, a little above Skylar to take advantage of the updraft, then Esther, Loomis and Weedle, each flying slightly behind and a little higher than the goose in front. Excitedly, he described the land they would fly over as if he had flown over it every day of his life. He swept his wings together and out again to illustrate wind currents and how the geese must make use of updrafts to conserve their energy.

"And there are *dangers,*" he concluded, his voice shaking dramatically, the surface of the pond trembling around him.

"Dangers . . . dangers," echoed Weedle, his wings raised, eyes rolling.

"Guns, foxes," Skylar honked over Weedle, "winds so fierce they fling you to the earth." He shuddered and the feathers rose all over his body. "Ice that can close on you like a trap." The flock shivered with Skylar. They were caught in the story now, believing him again. Weedle felt his small body pump up with each danger Skylar listed, as if he had already met and fended off each one himself.

Then, as Skylar's words trembled down to silence, the sun opened the sky a little wider and light flowed onto the pond. There was a moment of golden stillness. Then Skylar's call, "We're gone!" shot through the clear, bright air just as his wings thrust up and down, launching him from the surface of the pond. On the second stroke of his powerful wings, the others followed. The pond erupted in the wake of wings and the air thundered around them. The geese broke into a chorus of honking that awakened the people in the houses nearby. If they had happened to look out their windows at that moment, they would have seen a peculiar sight: two geese and a great blue heron rising from the sleeping neighborhood into the greatest adventure of their lives—and three geese floundering in the pond below.

CHAPTER 4
THE FIRST DAY'S JOURNEY

Skylar and Esther lifted off from the pond with all the ceremony the occasion called for. The other three made the same amount of noise and commotion, but it did not lift them off the surface of the pond. The frantic wing flapping from Roosevelt and Loomis raised such a wake in the pond it almost capsized Weedle behind them. Panicked at the sight of Skylar and Esther sailing effortlessly over the highway into the distance, the three left-behind geese lurched to the edge of the pond. In desperation, they began to run, flapping their wings with all their strength. Gradually, they gained the air. Flap by flap, they rose higher, then a little higher, until they cleared the road.

Except for Weedle. He could only manage to lift a few feet off the ground, then found himself teetering over the highway with a sixteen-wheeler bearing down on him. He yelped in terror, flapped his wings harder and harder as the truck grew larger and larger. Its front tires missed him by inches. The roar of tires and choke of exhaust fumes almost sent him plummeting onto the highway, but the truck's updraft caught the smallest goose and lifted him just high enough to gain his air balance. By strength of sheer will, Weedle thrust all his might into the act of flying. Gradually, very gradually, he gained the height of Roosevelt and Loomis, who were still far ahead of him.

Flying on with fierce determination, Roosevelt and Loomis and, finally, Weedle caught up to the two geese in the lead. Skylar and Esther, excited by their own thrilling ascent, did not look behind to see the bumbling assault of Roosevelt, Loomis and Weedle upon the air. None of the geese had seen Weedle's near collision with the truck.

The calamity of the takeoff was soon forgotten. The joy of lifting themselves on the strength of their own wings, the exhilaration of gaining height and belonging to the air above the ground, made the geese giddy with excitement. They felt wild—wild as any Canada goose ever felt. They shouted back and forth, soared and dove through the air, colliding gleefully with one another. The power of their untested wings amazed them.

Thirty feet behind flew the Who-on with solemn, effortless beats of his wings, legs stretched out against his body, neck folded upon his back.

"The formation! The formation!" Skylar shouted back at the geese. The flock scurried to find their formation while Skylar, honking commands in back of himself, flew straight into the top branches of a towering oak that crested a hill. Before he could catch his air balance, Skylar was plummeting down, through branch after branch of the oak. He struggled to regain the use of his wings, but his momentum carried him faster downward, until he landed with a *flumph* and squawk of indignation on the ground beneath the oak. The breath knocked out of him, he tumbled down the hill, feathers and webbed feet and wide-open beak, until finally he came to a stop in a little depression at the bottom. He was immediately joined by the flock of four fat geese, falling one by one behind him—in formation.

The Who-on alighted on the crown of the oak. He watched, mesmerized, as a single feather wafted down on the pile of geese. Slowly and with great difficulty, the geese untangled themselves from one another. When the geese had regained their composure and Skylar had stopped barking, the Who-on called down from his perch in the oak, "This is Lost Pond?" He studied what appeared to be a puddle near the pile of upside-down geese.

"Of course not!" honked Skylar, flapping his wings and shaking his tail feathers. "We just . . . stopped to think things over."

"Yes," huffed Roosevelt. "We always must first run into a tree, fall to the ground in a heap and make ourselves look perfectly ridiculous to do our best thinking-of-things-over."

Skylar glowered at Roosevelt.

As the geese inspected and adjusted their feathers, the Who-on turned his head and studied the puddle as if poised to pluck a bullfrog from its edges.

"Sorry to ruin the Who-on's meal prospects," announced Roosevelt after a while, "but I'm in need of a little dip." The Who-on twisted his head this way and that as he watched the portly goose waddle over to the edge. "If anyone cares to join me . . ."

The Who-on would have interrupted, but it was not easy to interrupt the geese. Besides, it often took him some time to come up with just the right way to make himself understood, so before he could tell Roosevelt that this was not a puddle at all, Roosevelt had discovered that for himself.

Loomis stared where Roosevelt had been.

The other geese stared, too.

All that remained of Roosevelt was a tiny Roosevelt-sounding voice coming from where the puddle was. Only it wasn't a puddle, as the Who-on would have told them if he could have gotten the words out. He swooped down from his perch to the edge and peered into a very deep hole in the ground. There was Roosevelt in the hole, which was really a natural cave, a thing the geese had never seen. The geese, led by Skylar, crept up cautiously behind the Who-on and peered down, too. Weedle gave a gasp as he shoved his head between the larger geese.

"Roosevelt is down a hole!" he shouted.

"Evidently," replied Skylar.

"Help," squeaked Roosevelt. He was balanced on a narrow ledge of the cave, his wings plastered against the stone wall. Below him was total darkness. He looked up at the geese and the Who-on looking down at him. He appeared very small and humble and un-Roosevelt-like.

"Fly out," offered Loomis. "You *can* fly, Roosevelt. Remember. We got here on wings."

Roosevelt said something back they couldn't hear.

"What?" shouted Skylar down to Roosevelt.

"I think he asked how," said Loomis.

"He can't fly out," said Esther. "See? There's not enough room for him to spread his wings."

"Well, *try*, Roosevelt!" ordered Skylar, annoyed by Esther's bad habit of being right.

Roosevelt began to hop a little on the ledge. He lifted his wings slightly as if he were going to fly, but this caused him to lose his balance and he flailed his wings frantically against the sides of the cave until he had regained his tenuous hold on the ledge. He gaped at the darkness below in horror.

The geese surrounding the hole began to realize one by one that Roosevelt was in a very unhappy predicament. He could not fly out, and geese cannot climb.

"What are we going to do?" Weedle asked Skylar. There followed a long silence.

"Leaving me here is *not* an option," came Roosevelt's anxious voice from below.

"Maybe the Who-on can help," Esther piped. The geese and the Who-on turned their attention from the hole to Esther. "Look how long he is!" she exclaimed. "All he has to do is lean down and stretch out his long neck and long beak and Roosevelt can clamp on and—"

"And the Who-on and Roosevelt can both be in the hole!" Skylar snapped.

Loomis and Weedle could not suppress a cackle at the thought of this.

"Not if we hold on to the Who-on," Esther argued.

The geese looked at one another. Roosevelt, they all knew, was no lightweight, and the chance of hauling him out of the hole was slim. But Esther's plan was their only plan. When the geese glanced over at the Who-on, the bird looked skeptical, though it was hard to tell, really, what he was thinking or if he was thinking. The geese were not at all sure the Who-on understood what they wanted him to do.

All at once but in slow motion, the heron leaned into the hole. Then he seemed to change his mind. He pulled himself upright again and stood for a long time looking off into the distance. He appeared to have forgotten about the geese, the hole, the journey. Then, in the same slow, deliberate way, he strode past the geese. Squawks of protest followed him, then fell silent as the geese watched the bird extend his long neck to pick up something out of the grass. It was a small branch, perhaps one that had broken off the oak they had all fallen through. He positioned it in his beak, then dropped it, chose another, pitched that one aside and selected another. Finally, with a stout branch about three feet long protruding from his beak, the Who-on stepped past the geese, who were watching him so intently none of them uttered a sound. Perched on the rim of the hole, the statuesque bird bent his long legs and leaned into it.

"Grab on, Roosevelt!" screeched Weedle, his voice careening off in excitement.

"Grab on," shouted Esther to Loomis in back of her. Then she clamped her beak onto the Who-on's tail feathers. Loomis, completely baffled, gazed at her a moment until it occurred to him that he should do the same.

"Grab on," he commanded Weedle, who already had a beak full of Loomis's tail feathers. Finally, with an exaggerated sigh, Skylar clamped onto Weedle.

Straining and puffing and losing a few tail feathers, the geese and the Who-on tugged and tugged until finally Roosevelt flopped up out of the hole with a grunt and snort, the branch clasped in his beak, a look of furious indignation in his eyes.

Once out of the hole, however, Roosevelt was Roosevelt again, without the slightest hint that he had ever had an anxious moment. He spit the branch out of his beak with a look of distaste and immediately went about the business of preening himself, as if the others were not there. First, he picked and pulled through the fine feathers on his breast, then he meticulously lifted and groomed each long flight feather. The Who-on studied Roosevelt with curiosity, then with one hop and two flaps of his wings, he was back on the top branches of the oak they had all fallen through.

"It's most inconvenient," Roosevelt said, looking accusingly up at the oak, "to carry on a migration with all this . . . vegetation . . . in the way!" Then, with a honk and shake of his tail feathers, he strutted away from the edge of the hole.

· · ·

After some debate back and forth about the nature of obstacles and, particularly, the nature of holes, the geese prepared to take flight again. The embarrassment of their clamorous fall from the sky and Roosevelt's fall into the earth was a fleeting cloud over their enthusiasm. Migrations are never easy, Skylar assured them as they lined up in their preflight formation. They were eager to continue their journey, to discover what other adventures awaited them on their first migration.

The Who-on observed the proceedings from the height of the oak. He did not understand these geese at all. Other geese, he suspected, spent less time complaining and thinking things over and more time in the air.

After several minutes of squawking and parading around, Skylar lowered his neck in takeoff stance. The others fell in behind him and soon the geese were airborne again. There was just as much noise and celebration as the first time. They flew north, into a bright sky, with the Who-on moving its great wings in what appeared to be slow motion compared to the vigorous flapping of the geese, thirty feet ahead.

· · ·

The celebration did not last long. The flock had hardly regained flying height when their formation began to fall apart. Esther had the habit of veering to the right and almost leaving the flock entirely. Weedle flew too low and nearly dropped out of sight, occasionally clamping onto Loomis's tail feathers for support. Loomis, however, provided little stability for Weedle. His long, floppy body lumbered through the air as if he were treading water. He either flew too high above the other geese, or dropped far below, slapping the air with his loose-jointed wings. A gasping Roosevelt, trying hard not to appear exhausted, bumped into Skylar repeatedly.

As for Skylar, his wings had become so heavy he was amazed each time they lifted. But to the fatigued geese behind him, he seemed to be flying with the reservoirs of strength of a goose born on the wing.

Skylar's ragged flock of four fat geese and one heron stopped many times during the first day's flight to think things over. The stops became more and more frequent, the landings and ascents more clumsy and contentious as the light of the day grew fainter. By the time the sun was drawing the sky behind it, they had lost all semblance of a flock, but had become five airborne acrobats and one attendant great blue heron who flew steadily, resolutely behind.

The geese strayed across the sky, dropping lower with each wing beat. They called weakly back and forth to one another, the universal call of geese: *"I am here . . . where are you?"* with Weedle yelping something piercing and unintelligible. Gradually, the call, like the formation, took many directions: *"I am here, but I don't know where that is"* and *"If I am here, then you can't be there"* and then *"I don't know where I am or where you are or where we're going or why we're going and isn't it time to land now?"*

Skylar honked until he was hacking, but the geese continued to straggle like an unstrung necklace across the sky. Abandoning all hope of collecting them into a flock and seeing they were steadily losing altitude, he decided to set the geese down in the midst of a cluster of mixed hardwoods and evergreens just ahead. Then his keen vision caught the edge of a mown cornfield just beyond the woods. His remembering light glowed within him. Wild geese often stopped in cornfields during their migrations. This one could not have happened along at a better time.

As loudly as he could manage, Skylar honked above the din of the squabbling geese, "Cornfield ahead . . . prepare to land," over and over again until his honking finally broke through their complaints. Focusing on "corn," the little group pulled together in the best impression of a flock they could manage, each barking excitedly, Weedle's high-pitched call adding a note of hysteria. The Who-on still followed, though he was not sure anymore what he was following.

The geese locked the cornfield in their sights and flew straight for it. But it seemed to come no closer. Each time their wings lifted, it was as if the air had turned solid. Just when the weight of the air against their wings seemed unbearable, the smallest goose, who lagged far behind the rest of the flock, fell from the sky, trailing bleating notes of panic. The Who-on made a quick stop in the topmost branches of a pine and watched Weedle's fall, a flurry of feathers tumbling head over heels through the sky. Then he observed a most peculiar phenomenon. As if all the geese were attached by an invisible line, one by one they followed Weedle's descent, until finally Skylar fell, too. It was the exact reverse of that morning's goose fall.

All five geese lay in a pitiful heap in the middle of a hemlock grove. Huddled there, they did not have the energy to complain or to think things over or, for that matter, even to move. It began to rain softly.

"This is a good, safe place to spend the night," came Esther's voice from somewhere inside the clump of feathers. "No eagles or foxes will think to look for us here," she said, as if they had chosen just the right place to land.

Very slowly and without a single indignant hiss or cackle, the geese got to their feet and began to methodically smooth their feathers back in place. Then, they slid their beaks beneath the coverlet of feathers on their shoulders, just as if it was any other evening back in their pond.

The first day had ended, though it had seemed like an entire migration had taken place in the course of a single day. Just before going to sleep himself, Skylar surveyed his flock of four. This was his habit, even in the pond they had come from, though only Esther was aware of it. She had often seen him do this. First, he looked to make sure Weedle was accounted for. Then the others. Everyone was safe. That, he thought, was a miracle. He scanned the horizon and the fast-closing night. Only with great effort did he spy the Who-on at the top of the pine. How does he do that? Skylar wondered. Become the missing part of everywhere he lands? Perhaps, he thought, *that* is what wildness really is. He wondered if his own ragged troop of overweight pond geese could ever learn belonging. This thought lay heavily upon him as he tucked his beak under his shoulder feathers and attempted to sleep.

CHAPTER 5
GEESE FROM THE NORTH

The geese awoke at the same time to the cold and hunger of a November morning. They shook the dampness from their wings and looked miserably in Skylar's direction. He answered with a hiss of irritation.

"The cornfield is not far," offered Esther, who was vigorously preening and shaking out her feathers as if she were preparing to take flight again. The other geese stared at her blankly, wings clamped close to their sides.

"It's just beyond these trees," she said. "We can fly there in no time and then we can feast on corn."

The words *feast* and *corn* roused the geese. They went about briskly preening themselves while arguing about the formation. Skylar barked a few times to remind them who was in charge, but only Weedle lifted his head and looked expectantly at him. The other geese were busy readying their feathers and their determination for flight.

Finally, the geese lined up in formation and assumed the preflight stance. They ran a few steps, honked loudly, stretched out their necks, flailed their wings, lifted a few feet off the ground, then plowed into the middle branches of the hemlocks that surrounded them. Hard as they tried, they could not gain enough height to clear the trees. With each new approach, they seemed to be bouncing rather than flying. Skylar, in the lead, climbed the highest, but he, too, faltered and fell down through the branches of the hemlocks, only to come out from under them spitting hisses, determined to try again.

Observing from above, the Who-on was baffled by all the up-and-down motion and squabbling that went on below him. Finally, after watching several minutes of wing flapping, honking and general commotion, the Who-on settled down amid the branches of the pine. *The geese must be thinking things over again*, he sighed to himself.

What was happening below was pandemonium among the geese. Upon experiencing the humiliation of no flight, after the humiliation of the goose fall from the sky, followed by Roosevelt's plunge into a hole he mistook for a puddle, Skylar lost his temper completely.

"Incompetents!" he blared as he emerged from the low branches of a hemlock after yet another failed takeoff attempt. "Four fat geese who can't even fly in formation. If you could fly in formation, we would be there by now. But no! You stray all over the sky, braying back and forth at one another like mules. What do you think other geese think of us!"

"And who was it that decided to take a bunch of fat geese on a migration anyway?" Roosevelt snorted.

"Who's fat?" squeaked Weedle.

"You are," said Roosevelt, turning his anger on Weedle. "We all are. We are geese who were meant for our nice, safe pond. We were meant to have our food brought to us. Our wings are just for show, not for flight!"

"But Skylar says—" protested Weedle.

"Skylar says, Skylar says," Roosevelt chided. "Words are not wings!"

"Yes," said Loomis uncertainly. "It's not as if we were *wild* geese."

"Of course not," Roosevelt said with a snap of his head. "We're not meant for this sort of thing at all. We're not like *him.*" He looked up to the tree-tops, until he spied the Who-on, who was looking down on the geese with his usual puzzled expression. Then the geese all began to squawk at once, until they forgot why they were squawking and only cared about who was loudest.

Finally, Esther said in a quiet voice that no one heard, "I'm too hungry to stay here arguing any longer." With that, she lowered her head and headed for the woods.

The other geese stopped squabbling. Watching her waddling off into the woods, the geese honked a goose laugh, which sounds like a loud human laugh squashed flat. Esther was certainly a comical sight as she plowed through the woods, pushing her way through the hemlock branches, belly sliding over fallen trees and scrambling under brush.

"She's walking!" cried Weedle in disbelief. Weedle turned to Skylar for an explanation, but Skylar only watched Esther as she disappeared into the woods, his head drawn back in an attitude of total surprise.

"How utterly . . . duckish," huffed Roosevelt, who had puffed himself up with indignation.

"So that's what we've come to!" exclaimed Loomis, imitating Roosevelt's outrage. Still, Skylar said nothing. Finally, he shook all the feathers on his body violently as if trying to fling off the entire episode. Then, with no further exhibition, he turned and followed where Esther had gone. Behind him scurried Weedle. The jeers and protests from Roosevelt and Loomis sputtered out. Then they, too, followed Esther, Skylar and Weedle into the woods.

The Who-on watched the goose parade with mounting bewilderment. When the geese reached the cornfield, he flew to the top of a maple at its edge. The crop had been harvested and the stalks cut, but the dried kernels and cobs left behind offered a feast scattered throughout the field. Not knowing what to say or whom to blame, the geese ate in silence.

All that day the geese alternately fed and rested. In the pond, they had never known what it was like to earn the need for food through flight. Now they knew. They were ravenously hungry.

It took the entire day to replenish the reserves of energy they would need for the next day's journey. When they had eaten enough to think of something else, they looked around and marveled at the world they had come into. It was big and restless and humming with energy and dangers that could be sensed but not seen. Nothing here was neatly arranged as it had been at the pond. There were no false figures of animals. No carpet-smooth lawn or lawn furniture. No highway or houses anywhere to be seen.

Skylar wondered if the geese looked as unnatural in this place as the plastic flamingos and ceramic frogs looked beside their pond back home. But the deer that stepped out of the woods into the field as the evening came on did not startle at the sight of the geese. The deer came every morning and evening to feed on the broken ears of corn and stalks before the snows covered the fields for the winter. They often came upon geese in the field and regarded the group only momentarily before dropping their heads to feed. This acceptance swelled the spirits of the little band of geese and they began to feel more and more sure they belonged in this place, amid the wide skies and bountiful fields. A gurgle of contentment rose in their throats, gathered into a chatter that occasionally lurched into piercing excitement that caused the deer to look up from their feeding.

As night came on, the colors of the geese feeding in the field blended into the colors of November, along with the deer, the rain-darkened earth flecked with snow, the bleached cornhusks and stubble of mown stalks.

When the geese awoke the next morning, the rain had retreated and a quiet light eased through the remaining leaves of maples and beech. Everything glistened and welcomed. November had always been an empty season for the geese, a month of leaving, when all color and life were swept away with the fall migrations. This year, they were part of the going. They saw November in a new light. It was a light that flowed through each of them. They all felt it, though none of the geese knew it for what it was: the remembering light, which showed brightest in November.

"Look," called out Esther suddenly. The geese and even the deer raised their heads. A flock of geese were approaching from the north. Esther sounded the distance call to the geese. They called back, setting off a ruffle of excitement in the little flock on the ground.

"They answered," Esther whispered to herself.

The pond geese stared in awe at the approaching flock, their perfect V formation stenciled against the sky. When they were almost overhead, the flock broke out of formation, turned against the wind to slow their ascent, then hailed down upon the field in a storm of wings and calling. The pond geese drew closer together, bracing themselves against the great rollicking wave of calls as the wild geese swept across the field like a wind from other places.

None of the pond geese made a sound or move. Watching these geese descend from the sky as if delivered of it rocked their confidence. They clustered at the other end of the field, their necks low to the ground in an attitude of intimidation. They felt small and unworldly among the magnificent birds who were familiar with the flight patterns, the cycles and seasons across the globe. But at least the pond geese knew that even if they were not as worldly as the wild geese, they were not statues in a pond either.

"That's the point goose," whispered Weedle excitedly to Skylar. "He came in ahead of all the others. Did you see? They all waited for him to land first! He's the point goose, like you, Skylar. Right?" The word *right* sprang up to an ear-piercing pitch.

Skylar grunted in reply and moved away from the yelping Weedle to separate himself slightly from association with the pond geese. He watched the wild geese intently. The others, too, studied the wild geese as they moved through the fields, efficiently prodding the earth for kernels of corn.

"The places they must have seen," whispered Esther.

"The mountain ranges," said Loomis, "the forests . . . the *dangers.*"

They had not noticed Weedle slip away from their group and waddle up to a large gander who stood with neck erect at the edge of the cornfield.

"I just want to know," said Weedle, hopping up to catch the eye of the gander, who was looking over him, "how you keep it all straight."

The pond geese behind Weedle gawked in embarrassment.

The gander, who was the sentinel for the flock, arched his neck like a bow at Weedle, opened his beak wide, stuck out his tongue and hissed. Weedle stopped hopping. Skylar moved in protectively behind the small goose, looking over Weedle's head directly into the eyes of the sentinel.

"I just want to know," Weedle said in a squeaky, tentative voice. The sentinel, who had flinched slightly at Skylar's gaze, straightened his neck again and cocked his head at Weedle, as if trying to decide what manner of fowl was addressing him. "How you geese fly at night without bumping into one another," Weedle finished nervously.

Now some of the other wild geese, those closest to the edge of the field where the sentinel stood watch, stopped their feeding to listen. They made low-pitched, rumbling noises in their throats, and the pond geese suspected the wild geese were mocking Weedle's ignorance. Finally, one drew away from the others and came up behind the sentinel, who still had not answered, but glanced from Weedle to Skylar in frank distrust.

"You're not wild geese, are you?" asked the goose, who was not much larger than Weedle.

Weedle was surprised by the goose's voice, which was so different in pitch he did not quite understand what was being asked. Finally, the words settled into place for him.

"Oh, but we want to be," he burst out in his excited falsetto voice. The wild goose recoiled its neck a little and looked at Weedle in bewilderment.

Esther stepped out from behind Skylar and stood beside Weedle. "We have spent most of our lives raised by people," she explained. "We come from a pond just south of here."

"South?" interrupted a burly goose in back of the one who had been speaking. This set off a ripple of clucks and cackles among the geese. "That's the wrong way!"

"We know . . . of course . . . we're . . . uh . . . ," sputtered Esther, turning her attention back to the smaller goose in front of her. "We are . . . escorting . . ." She looked around. The Who-on was nowhere to be seen, and the wild geese were looking at her as if she were a plastic flamingo. Suddenly, their migration seemed as misguided as Roosevelt was always saying. "We are flying north to join another flock," she said, recovering herself at last, "before migrating south." The geese looked at her sideways. "It's a long story," she sighed. "Anyway, this is our first migration, and we do not know very much about it."

Skylar pushed past Weedle and Esther. "It is *their* first migration. I am trying to make something of it." The wild geese made the low rumbling noises in their throats.

"Do you tell the way by the stars?" Esther asked, squeezing in front again. "I heard that is the way to tell."

"By stars and by cornfields, mountain ranges, valleys and the way rivers go," replied the wild goose. The other geese behind the one speaking seemed to carry on a barely audible undercurrent of conversation, though their attention was trained on the pond geese.

"By the sun?" piped Weedle from behind the other two geese. He had heard Skylar say this.

"Yes, by the sun, too," answered the wild goose.

"Sometimes, it is all these things," replied another goose with the same dark coloring and dusky markings as Esther. Speaking seemed to take a great effort for the dark goose. He quickly turned his attention away, thrusting his beak into the dark earth for kernels of corn.

"Each goose is born with the way imprinted on its memory," said another goose, joining the others. "Each time you use it, it grows stronger, like your wings."

"But how do you know when it's one thing or another thing that shows the way?" asked Esther. She was following the goose who resembled her so closely she nearly collided with him when he turned to answer her.

"You are a goose. You will know. It is inside you to know."

"And the dangers?" Esther began, but then her courage failed. She was suddenly afraid of the answer.

"Dangers are everywhere along the migration," the goose said with a hint of sternness. "A live goose is a wary goose. You must see danger before it sees you."

"But . . . how?"

"You are a goose. You will know," the goose repeated wearily, and turned back to feeding.

In the next instant the sentinel goose swung his neck around, setting into motion a wave of heads sweeping toward the skies. Into gray light from the north, more geese were arriving. The Canada geese sounded a distance call, and the approaching geese answered. It is the universal way with geese to connect to one another, even though it was clear as the geese came nearer that they were not Canada geese. The new arrivals were greylag geese, handsome gray geese almost as large as the Canadas. They glided out of the skies, webbed feet spread out before them, and landed on the run. They spread across the field before pulling themselves together into their flock. All the geese continued to call back and forth, keeping voice contact though they did not mingle.

"Hunters . . . and a hailstorm far to the north," Esther said in a tremulous voice, her eyes wide with fear.

"What?" asked Skylar. When he turned to Esther, she had gone rigid in alarm.

"These other geese—" she gasped. "I cannot understand everything they say." She closed her eyes tightly and leaned her whole body in the direction of the new arrivals. "They come from much farther north. Almost at the top of the world. They are telling of dangers . . . hunters and terrible storms. . . ."

"Dangers. Enough of dangers!" Skylar honked back, dismissing all thought of danger with a sweep of his wings.

"But didn't you hear," she said breathlessly, "what the wild goose said? We must be wary. We must see danger before it sees us."

"Esther, you sound like Roosevelt. Dangers, dangers everywhere," he mimicked.

"Roosevelt is right," she blurted out, fear flaring in her eyes as she listened to the conversations of the new arrivals. "Wild geese are hunted geese. Hunted by guns, by hunger, by foxes, by storms."

"So," exclaimed Skylar, "you are afraid, too!"

Esther looked at Skylar as if he had just come into focus. "Yes," she replied. "I thought I had flown beyond my fears, but here they are again." Esther dropped her head. She was struggling with an enemy inside herself.

"Well," announced Skylar, strutting around Esther as if he were delivering a sermon, "I fear nothing. Let danger come. I will fly right through it!"

Esther raised her head as if Skylar had just said something important. Then she seemed to sink deep into her own thoughts again, her entire body compressing until she looked much smaller than she was. Skylar grunted and marched off, looking for another goose to impress.

All the wild geese were very tired and very hungry, and soon the circle of their contact calls grew tighter and tighter until they were confined to each individual family group. There were ten families of geese all flying together to destinations along the Atlantic coast. They had over two thousand miles more to fly.

The geese had spread out over the entire field, but now that it grew darker they pulled together, away from the wooded edges. Skylar's small flock lingered near them, eager to know more about their migration, but the geese were clearly not inviting further conversation.

Skylar's flock spent the rest of the evening guessing the places the wild flock had been to and seen, and the dangers they had met and overcome. They watched their movements closely—the way the geese meticulously preened themselves, the little dips and stretches and circular motions of their necks that composed another kind of language, the many dialects they spoke in their intimate family groups that could barely be understood by the pond geese.

Finally, as the lights went out on the day, the wild geese tucked their beaks under their shoulder coverlets and slept.

"Just like us," said Weedle with satisfaction.

While the geese communed in the field, the Who-on flew overhead, searching the land below for a promising pond. He found one behind the barn near the field where the geese had landed. With his long beak and gift for patience, the Who-on probed the small pond for fish and mud-buried salamanders and frogs. After he had eaten what the pond had to offer, he flapped his large wings and soared to the top of a hemlock and settled into it as if he were its crown. He scanned the field below. The geese had all nestled down for the night. He could see, though, that one goose in the large flock remained with his head up while the others slept. It was the sentinel. Separate from the large flock of geese was Skylar's flock, who slept with their heads burrowed into their wing feathers as if the dangers they had heard of throughout the day belonged to another landscape. The Who-on watched them long after the sun traded light with the moon.

Sometime during the night, Skylar's flock was awakened by a thunder crack of wings as both flocks of wild geese departed the field. Each of the pond geese felt a strong tug in their breasts as they watched the wild geese fly across the moon. The honking of the wild geese could be heard even after they were no longer visible in the sky. *"I am here . . . where are you?"* they called. All the pond geese understood this call, if they could not completely understand the language of the other geese. They sent it back across the distance again and again until the words hung there in the wide, unanswering sky.

CHAPTER 6
THAT WHICH SLITHERS AND SNARLS AND STALKS

The first light of dawn was dimmed by a thin, slanting rain, but the geese, as if by signal, lifted their heads at exactly the same time, stretched their necks and shook themselves. They worked their beaks through their feathers quickly, and within minutes they were lined up and ready for flight. This time they did not argue about the formation. They did not ask how far Lost Pond was. Even Loomis and Weedle managed not to jostle and taunt each other.

This morning, Skylar observed, they were a different flock. Perhaps the wild geese had left them with more wisdom and determination. Perhaps they saw the possibility of reaching their destination. They stood ready and confident. Not a squabble, yelp, whine or whimper issued from the group.

Skylar stopped himself from barking the usual preflight instructions. Instead, he simply rose into the air. The others followed, feeling strength rise in their wings like sap up the trunk of a maple tree in early spring. There was joy in their call as they reached their flying height, clicked into formation and spread across the sky in an almost perfect check mark.

The call of the geese echoed between November hills. No one would guess that the flock flying like a wedge in the sky three thousand feet above were anything but wild geese. The last of the fall migrations. Winter would be close behind.

The world below bloomed quietly into focus. The rain brought out the earth's inside colors—the sea green of lichen-covered stone, lush mosses, leaf casings, the here-and-there brightness of late fallen leaves. Deer, the exact tone of tree trunks, appeared then vanished instantly, as if taken back inside the trees. Bodies of water swelled and glittered beneath them. The world was a beautiful place.

Behind them, with great solemn flaps of his wings, flew the Who-on, who had been almost completely forgotten by the geese.

The geese were lifted on an updraft that enabled them to glide along almost effortlessly, flapping their wings only intermittently for long periods of time. In this way, they were able to keep their formation intact for almost the entire day, calling back and forth to one another constantly—"*I am here . . . where are you?*"—while the earth was remade beneath them. There were fewer roads and squares of yards and houses. The world swelled with greenness. It was a land thick with hemlock forests, strong with granite cliffs, fast running with many streams and rivers and deep with valleys, cradling lakes surrounded by nothing but more wildness.

On and on they flew, feeling the surge of the updraft as if the earth itself were breathing, lifting the geese on each exhale. When Skylar grew tired in the lead, Esther, without asking, without telling, pulled ahead of him and took the point. Loomis and Weedle argued back and forth about when it would be their turn to lead, but Roosevelt threw back the stern reply that they were both too young and inexperienced to lead and if anyone should be leading it was he, though, of course, he was not one to push the issue.

While in the lead, Esther unexpectedly began an ascent, up to the height of a soaring hawk. Though the geese followed more or less in formation behind her, they all complained about the sudden change, just when flying was going so well. They continued to complain until she had brought them up to a thermal and they all rode on the strong back of a swifter current.

"Hey," exclaimed Roosevelt, "I don't have to flap at all now."

"Look, loose-stuff," cried Weedle, "I'm an eagle." At this, Loomis clamored on top of Weedle and the two of them wrestled until they tumbled off the back of the thermal and had to struggle to climb back on.

"Humph," said Skylar. "See what trouble you cause, Esther, when you change things!" But he himself could not help but be exhilarated by the new height and speed. Gradually, the geese settled down to enjoy the lift under their outstretched wings for as long as the current would carry them. Finally, they slid off the end of it all the way down to their former flying level, where the Who-on still flew steadily on.

. . .

The third night the geese flew until almost night-fall in search of a safe place to land. The earth below was bundled into forested mountains. Feeling his flock grow weary and disjointed, Skylar chose to land in a pond nestled deep in the hollow where two mountains joined. A little island, probably formed over an abandoned beaver lodge, rose from the middle of the pond and provided a good view to approaching dangers. There appeared to be very little to eat here, but it was the safest place to land that they had come upon in hours of flying. Still, the pond struck fear in Skylar's heart. Ice was stitching its trap along the shores of the water. He had avoided landing on ponds because of his early memory of being trapped by ice, but the forest harbored endless possibilities of dangers and was too dense for a safe landing and takeoff. Skylar circled the pond many times. Circling and hovering was not easy for the tired, out-of-shape geese, and they wobbled and careened unsteadily in the air before Skylar gave the signal to land. Esther and Roosevelt, and the Who-on flying behind them, wondered what had taken him so long to give the signal, when clearly the geese were too tired to fly any farther.

The exhausted geese honked their contact call as they skidded across the pond to break their speed, tearing the thin veil of ice with their large webbed feet. They made so much noise landing that it took several minutes for the silence and water to settle around them. Then they scanned the shoreline. Darkness gathered there in many shapes and forms, shapes that could be anything. Each goose's heart beat faster at the terrifying vision of snarling, slithering or stalking predators. Finally, their fears quieted, too, and they gathered underneath thickets of dogwood berry bushes that grew in the midst of the little island.

Skylar's fear, which he would never reveal to the others, was of another predator. A predator that did not snarl, slither or stalk. It did not bear guns. It was the ice, the ice that came on as silently as the night. His fear kept him separate and vigilant.

He gave a little jump when Esther approached him. Afraid she had noticed his nervousness, he puffed himself up to look as big and fearless as possible. Esther did not seem to notice the display. She had something on her mind.

"Skylar," she said, excitement percolating in her eyes, "I've been thinking about what you said. And you are right!"

Skylar looked confused.

"What you said about fear. I've been thinking about it. It was fear that kept me from flying; fear that kept us all in that pond. It is the biggest danger we face. We must never let it overtake us again. We must always fly ahead of it."

Skylar did not remember that he had said all that, but he nodded knowingly. He was about to have more to say on the subject of fearlessness when he noticed Esther's eyes dart to something in back of him. Skylar swung his attention around to where Esther was staring. Moonlight flashed off two pairs of eyes, and the darkness took the shape of two raccoons poised at the edge of the little island, their eyes fixed on the geese. All Skylar's alarms went off. Fear of ice had taken the form of raccoons. His eyes bulged, his tongue jutted out of his open beak, his wings flew up. The other geese were roused out of their slumber by the blaring noise of Skylar's attack call, the snarling of the raccoons and the great thrashing blows of Skylar's wings. They stumbled awake, hissing and honking, their necks lowered as they formed a half circle behind Skylar.

The raccoons, who hadn't wanted a fight in the first place, backed into the water and swam to the shore of the pond, where they immediately disappeared into the thick underbrush, leaving Skylar huffing at the edge of the island.

Finally, assured of his victory, Skylar swung around to face the geese, who greeted him with the triumph call and dance, a ceremony geese perform in honor of a conqueror. Though he tried to look annoyed by the elaborate display of honking, twirling and high stepping, the feathers rose all over Skylar's body.

"You are very brave, Skylar," Esther said with a little dip of her head. Behind Esther's quiet praise, Weedle jumped up and down in such a frenzied dance both his body and voice bounced out of control. Skylar stepped over to Weedle and placed his wing tip lightly on his bouncing head until the little goose slowly came to a stop and gazed with dazed admiration up at Skylar. Gently, Skylar nudged Weedle in close to the others.

After the geese had finally settled down again, Skylar remained alert. It was not the returning

raccoons he was listening for, but for the advance of his mortal enemy, ice. Now, in the deepest part of the night, Esther's words glowed inside him. Fear, he understood, is danger, too. Out of fear, other fears grow and spread like fire. Skylar knew that as leader, he must not let fear overtake him. He shivered, feeling the cold breath of fear. Mists dragged through the blackened pines. The low, sorrowful tones of owls dipped into the darkness. He watched the sky, hoping for the reassuring sight of wild geese or the profile of the heron against the sky. It was with great relief that he noticed Esther awaken. She looked over at Skylar, dipped her head, then alertly scanned the sky. Feeling relieved of his post, Skylar fell heavily to sleep.

CHAPTER 7
THE STORM

The geese had flown almost two hundred miles. It had taken them much longer than it would have taken wild geese to fly the same distance, but the pond geese did not know that. In fact, they were very proud of themselves, individually and as a flock. And they were proud of Skylar for guiding them into their first real migration.

There were many things that they were not aware of, though, things wild geese know. They were not aware how quickly storms can come on or how fortunate they had been, so far, to escape disaster. Somewhere to the north were gunshots, but they seemed very distant now. Distant as their former lives. The strength was surging into their wings, and they were learning to use the pressure of the air under their flight feathers to manipulate the wind currents to lift, to turn, to descend. They played the minor variations of thermals and updrafts with their wing tip fingers. Even Weedle and Loomis seemed to understand how their wings worked with the wind and when to flap and when not to flap, though Loomis seemed always to be floundering in the air like a goose drowning in sky.

The geese listened to one another now, at least most of the time, instead of each trying to honk louder than the other. They listened and understood the signals that passed from one goose to the other that told them to fly higher or lower, or when to land.

On the fourth day of their journey, the five Canada geese and one great blue heron rose out of the shadow of the hills to meet the sun. All fear was left on the shores of the beaver pond. They soared into a ringing clear sky, its very blueness buoying their wings as they exploded into the sky and clicked into formation. It was a day made for them.

A large body of water shimmered into view, and beyond rose mushrooming formations of cumulonimbus clouds. The geese locked the lake in their memories, but the cloud formations, though they appeared as solid as a mountain range, would vanish with the next weather front. Clouds, geese knew, were the fourth dimension, after land, water, sky. A country of clouds now lay ahead of them—very far or very near—chambered, luminous, inviting.

Without realizing it, Skylar, at the point, began to fly faster, heading directly for the clouds, as if cloud country were the destination. The other geese followed closely, keeping a tight formation, as if they, too, were rushing toward their destination.

Suddenly, they were inside the clouds that had seemed so far away, flying through chamber after chamber of cloud density. They flew through blue light, no light, yellow light and then into the blinding light as they broke out of the clouds into the bright sky. The geese passed from one cloud into another, sometimes losing sight of one another entirely.

This was great fun for Weedle, who had a vivid imagination and highly developed sense of fun. To him, each cloud he entered was like discovering a new sky kingdom, a kingdom he somersaulted through in blind glee, tumbling out the other side.

"Weedle! You're out of formation! What about the formation?" Loomis called back to the air-tumbling goose behind him, but Weedle was having too much fun to answer. Loomis tried to keep focused on the effort of flying in sync with the geese ahead, just behind and above Roosevelt, but soon he, too, lost concentration. Giving in to the temptation to join the fun, Loomis broke out of formation and soon both geese were rolling beak over webbed feet through the clouds, falling out of the bottom into the blue sky, while the rest of the flock flew on, mindless of them.

Loomis gave a shriek of panic when he finally quit tumbling and caught sight of the rest of the flock, specks in the sky ahead, disappearing into a bank of clouds. "They're almost out of sight!" gasped Loomis. "Hurry up, Weedle," he called back over his shoulder as he struggled to gain altitude. Weedle, however, saw no reason to hurry. He had just fallen out of a cloud and was wondering why the bottom of the cloud did not tear open when he fell through it. He was so absorbed by this question, he tried again and again to make the clouds tear behind him. Loomis gave one more contact call to Weedle, then lunged ahead, beating the air in a frantic attempt to catch up to the others.

Fear began to gather in each of the three geese ahead as they sensed a change in the air pressure. Something bad was coming, and coming fast. The translucent blue of the sky hardened into a metallic gray. The radiant country that had been so inviting began to close around them. Within minutes, the air temperature dropped, and the wind that had supported the geese in flight shifted direction. Suddenly, they were flying against it.

"Storm," cried Esther from behind Skylar at about the same instant that Skylar realized it, too.

"Storm!" bellowed Roosevelt.

"Storm?" asked the breathless Loomis, who had just caught up with the other geese.

Wild geese would have known with the first shade of dullness in the sky, the first hint of change in the air pressure and temperature, and in many other intuitive ways that a storm was coming. Wild geese would have landed long before the pond geese uttered the word *storm*.

It happened very fast. The clouds compressed and locked them in, shutting off the view of the land below. The geese flew on in a shadowed void. They could not fly above or below the thickening clouds. They would have to land quickly, and blindly. But what was below them? Skylar tried to remember the landforms they had flown over. The lake. He remembered it glittering beneath them, but then what? He had been mesmerized by the cloud formations ahead, drawn to them by some powerful force. He had failed to track landmarks. When he tried to dip below the clouds to search for a landing place, the wind, hurling icy rain now, slammed against him and the other geese.

"We must land!" wheezed Roosevelt. He bobbed in the air, his wings blown upward like a broken umbrella.

"But . . . where is—" Before Skylar could finish his words, the wind tore them away and flung its full force against the geese. They were puppets of the wind now, keeping just enough control of their wings to remain aloft. The wind had stolen their power of flight.

Contact calls snapped and frayed. All connections between the geese were broken, snatched away by the storm. The geese were deaf, blind, helpless. One instant they were thrown laterally; the next they were falling, falling, then lifted, then falling again. It seemed they were prisoners of the storm for hours when, in fact, it was less than two minutes before the geese were released by the storm and flung to earth.

They could have landed anywhere—on the sharp, jutting outcropping of a cliff, in the middle of a lake, in the jaws of a coyote, in a hunter's sights—but the storm surprised them again. It dropped them in a place they might have chosen to roost for the night. They were deposited, one by one, amid a forest of black spruce, with wide, sheltering branches.

Skylar landed first and quickly scrambled under the spreading boughs of the nearest spruce.

"*I am here . . . ,*" came his call tentatively out of the icy rain and darkness. For a long time, there was no answer. "*I am here,*" he repeated forcefully into the raging shadows. As he searched the gloomy darkness, he was gradually able to make out the shape of a goose in front of him.

It was Esther, standing only feet away. She stared straight at him but did not seem to see him.

"Esther," he shouted. "This way." She seemed unable to move until Roosevelt landed not far from her, jolting her out of her trance of terror.

"*I am here*—at least until I'm blown over there!" snorted the fat goose as he bowled his way past Esther, thumping the back of her head with his wing. "And you are, too, Esther, whether you want to be or not. Get a move!"

"I am here . . . ?" Esther asked in a thin, wavering voice as Roosevelt ushered her along in front of him. Within seconds, the three were huddled under the spruce, listening intently for the calls of the others. It seemed a very long time before they heard the flat *ker-honk* of Loomis. The frightened goose called so incessantly he couldn't hear the answering call of the other geese. He staggered around in the darkness bellowing until his voice finally cracked and gave out. Then he caught the tail end of a contact call. Then the full *"I am here . . . where are you?"* first from Skylar, then from Roosevelt, then from Esther. With an emphatic flap of his wings, he followed the calls to the spruce and happily scrambled under the boughs to where the other geese were gathered.

The geese kept close to one another, and for a long time they were absolutely silent while the spruce trees roared above them. Suddenly, the wind that had tormented them for hours fell silent. It would gather its strength, like a cougar after the hunt, and return, but for now it allowed a plaintive call to waft out from beneath the branches of the spruce.

"*Weedle . . . Weedle . . . where are you?*" Loomis called over and over until the storm returned and ushered his call away.

CHAPTER 8
THE CANYON WITH THE RIVER GONE

As wild geese know, storms are unpredictable. They can pounce in an instant or gather for hours. While the front of the storm hit the flock of geese head-on, its tail end whipped around to give the smallest goose trailing far behind the ride of his life. Weedle gladly traded his power of flight to ride the wind. He was swept up and away on its currents, cradled for a few seconds before he was sent looping through the air, then caught again and swept along for another few seconds before the wind, as if tired of the game, abandoned him.

The next thing he knew, he was bumping along on his rear end across the rocky bottom of a very narrow river valley between two steep walls of stone. In the spring, a mountain-fed stream fattened into a river that filled this canyon. In this season, it contained only the loss of the river. Weedle looked around at the absence about him. The first thing he thought was, *Where are the other geese?* The second thing was, *I'm hungry.* The third thing he thought, looking up the steep stone cliffs and discovering he was in a canyon, was, *This isn't fun anymore.*

He could not simply fly out of the canyon. The walls were too steep and narrow. Only very strong wings could generate the burst of power needed to make the steep ascent. Weedle's attempts only bounced him against the cliff, sending him sprawling back to the canyon floor.

"*I am here,*" called Weedle, from where he landed on his fifth attempt, amid the branches of a stunted cedar growing out of the canyon wall. But his feeble call came echoing back to him off the stone and absence that surrounded him.

My call can't even get out of here, thought Weedle. *How am I going to?*

He poked his beak into moss, lichen, fern, barren black raspberry bushes, pebbles. Nothing there for a goose to eat. As he searched through the sparse vegetation and stones of the valley floor, a very large and peculiar shadow passed over him and disappeared into the shadows of the canyon walls.

"The Who-on?" Weedle gasped, looking up. He jumped up and down with anticipation of rescue, but the shadow that passed did not come again. Neither did the geese. Where had the wind taken them? wondered Weedle. Had they flown on to Lost Pond without him? The sun was rising up the canyon wall, pulling the darkness behind it. It would be a clear night. A cold night. The storm had passed.

The moon shifted its white gaze onto the canyon floor, finding Weedle there. Feeling exposed to predators, the little goose scurried under the stunted cedars, the only shelter the canyon offered. Before he gave up on being rescued for the night and settled down to sleep, the thought occurred to him that his first migration might be his last migration. This so alarmed the little goose that he let out one last long, piercing contact call. He comforted himself with the belief that his call had risen higher than the canyon walls and found its way to his flock.

. . .

In his dream, Loomis was not a long, loose goose thrashing across the sky in search of a wind current to jump onto, but a sleek, wild goose who flew with strong, even beats of his wings. He was a goose who had flown the Atlantic flyway from the South Pole to the North Pole.

In his dream, Skylar kept a true course into and out of storms. His vision burned through the clouds, and he never lost sight of land or wavered in certainty that he was going in the right direction.

In her dream, Esther soared above fear. It had no hold on her.

In his dream, Roosevelt floated like a big balloon on an updraft that never required him to use his wings and never let him down.

And in each of their dreams, they were all flying in search of Weedle. In each of their dreams, they answered the contact call of the smallest goose.

As soon as needles of light pierced through the branches of the spruce, the geese were up and prepared to lift off, each determined to find Weedle, each pointed in the same direction.

"Not that way," came a voice from behind them.

It was the Who-on. None of the geese had seen the Who-on since before the storm. In fact, for many miles, they had not even thought about the Who-on flying behind them like a shadow. They had even forgotten that the Who-on was the reason for this great adventure. Now the big bird, who seemed to belong wherever he landed, bobbed awkwardly on the low limb of a spruce. He looked a little out of place and a little out of sorts.

"How do you know?" snorted Roosevelt. "You have no sense of direction, after all."

"I saw where the storm dropped him," replied the Who-on in the same calm, almost bored, tone. "The little one. I saw him between two stone cliffs, far, far down."

The Who-on's eye had caught only a glimpse of the white marking on Weedle's face as he had glided over, but he knew instantly that a goose in a canyon could only be one of the pond geese. He was becoming less and less surprised by the habits of these geese whose pond he had landed in four days ago. They seemed to take more time squabbling than flying, more time thinking things over than figuring things out and more time down than up.

"And it's not the way you are pointing," he said. "It's back that way." The Who-on twisted his long neck to look in back of himself. "I'm sure of it," he said, not sure of it at all.

Skylar shook out his wings and paced around, looking troubled and confused. "The storm must have blown us off course. So the way we were going seems like the way we came and—"

"You're not suggesting we follow the Who-on, who doesn't know here from there?" snorted Roosevelt.

"But he was the last to see Weedle," Loomis blurted out. The geese became agitated, plucking at their breast feathers, shaking their heads and making anxious, clucking sounds. None of the geese wanted to fly back the way they had come. Every hour lost was another hour that winter advanced upon them. They could feel its icy breath. The storm had left a fine coating of snow over the branches of the spruce. They looked to Skylar for an answer.

"We will find Weedle," he said back to them with his usual Skylar-like authority, though he had no idea how this would happen.

The geese looked at him questioningly. "I'll go back with the Who-on," announced Skylar, stretching his neck to its full height. Once again the power of his own words had overtaken him. He became Skylar the Rescuer. He saw himself lifting Weedle out of the canyon on his back, rising up out of the depths, the sun glistening off his wings. The other geese would receive them in a circle of admiration. A triumph dance would follow.

"No," said Esther, deflating Skylar the Rescuer. "We will all go. It is too dangerous to be separated." Esther looked rigid with determination. It was the first time she had spoken since the contact call of the night before.

"But if Skylar *wants* to go—" said Roosevelt.

"Esther's right," said Loomis. "We are a flock. We stick together."

The geese stared back at Loomis, who was sounding more like Skylar than Skylar, who had gone sullenly quiet.

And it was not Skylar who was first in the air to follow the Who-on. It was Loomis. He flopped and flailed his way to the point, looking like the effort would shake him to pieces, but soon he caught a wind current and his wing flaps, though loose and ungainly still, found a rhythm of their own and propelled him through the sky on the back of the wind. It did not bother Loomis that, technically, he was following the Who-on and not "leading." In his mind, he was the goose he had been in his dream. He was at the point and he remained there until he and the other geese began to wonder if, after all, the Who-on knew where he was taking them.

"Just like I thought!" roared Roosevelt after what seemed hours of flying. "We're following a one-eyed heron with no sense of direction on a wild-goose chase!"

But before Roosevelt could gather the breath for another complaint, the Who-on and Loomis were circling to land.

CHAPTER 9
THE RESCUE

At first they did not see nor hear him. He was deep in the shadows of the canyon, and his call was too weak to make it all the way up to the geese who peered down the canyon walls into the darkness.

"Are you sure he's there?" asked Loomis.

"Unless something's eaten him," replied the Who-on casually.

"What?" sputtered Loomis in alarm. "*Weedle . . . I am here. . . . Where are you?*"

Weedle saw the geese and the heron but could not make them see him. His call could not reach.

"*I am here. . . . I am here!*" he called over and over, but still the geese peering down into the canyon could not see him there nor hear him.

"Are you sure this is the right canyon?" asked Skylar. In fact, the Who-on was not at all sure until he turned his head at just the right angle and caught the movement of something far below.

"Yes," he replied, "quite sure."

Then the geese saw, too, and began honking at the top of their lungs and jumping up and down. Weedle, far below, did the same, but after the honking and jumping, he was still trapped in the canyon.

The geese stared down and Weedle stared up. A small, cold wind ruffled the feathers of the geese at the top of the canyon. Before yesterday, they would have thought it an innocent enough wind, but now they sensed it was the advance of another storm.

"No use," said the heron flatly. The geese glared at him, but the Who-on only cocked his head and looked back at them.

"You propose we leave him here?" said Skylar.

The Who-on simply blinked back at Skylar, his golden eye revealing nothing.

"The longer we stay here . . . ," said Roosevelt, shaking his head gravely.

"WE CAN'T LEAVE HIM HERE!" blared Loomis, forcing Roosevelt a few steps back.

Roosevelt recovered with an infuriated hiss. He brushed Loomis aside to address Skylar. "You are the self-proclaimed leader of this herd of honkers. Leaders sometimes have to make choices . . . difficult choices."

"We didn't choose to leave you down that hole you managed to get yourself into!" snapped Esther. Her words were strong, but she knew that Roosevelt was right. A difficult choice might have to be made for the sake of the flock. And she, more than any of the other geese, felt the threat of a storm in the wind that was coming up stronger now.

"We can't leave Weedle," whimpered Loomis. His determination was deflating as he felt less and less support from the others, who surrounded him in gloomy silence. The Who-on cocked his head as if waiting for them to come to the inevitable decision.

"And we won't," interjected Skylar. He broke through the circle of geese and strode to the edge of the cliff. He jerked his head up, then down with a sharp, decisive motion. As the astonished geese looked on, he plunged from light into darkness, as if he had fallen to the bottom of the world.

Skylar himself was not sure why he did it. It might have been for Weedle. It might have been for the sake of Skylar the Rescuer, but either way he was descending fast. He had to backpedal frantically to keep from sprawling onto the canyon floor. As it was, his landing was far less glorious than he had imagined.

Weedle began bouncing excitedly as Skylar plopped, skidded, thumped and landed on his breast in front of him. He continued to bounce until slowly the bounces became shorter and shorter. Finally, he stopped completely and asked, "Skylar, how is you being down here going to get me up there?"

In fact, Skylar was not at all sure how two geese at the bottom of a canyon was any better than one goose at the bottom of a canyon. His word power failed him. He tried to recover the vision of Skylar the Rescuer.

"I'm going to help you fly out of here," he said without very much conviction.

"But, Skylar, I don't have the wing power—"

"Yes, you do," Skylar answered with a snap of his head. "Right here." With the tip of his wing, Skylar tapped Weedle's pectoral muscles, which propel the wings, and deeper still, the heart, which propels the muscle. "You can fly out of here." Skylar's words seemed to step out ahead of him again. Behind the bold words, Skylar was not at all sure that Weedle could manage the sharp ascent out of the canyon.

Weedle studied the canyon walls, the bright patch of sky and the tiny heads bobbing at the top of the canyon, high, high above. "I can?"

"You have to," said Skylar. The darkness was creeping up the stone walls, and a snaking wind, howling *ooo-eee-ooo,* whipped through the canyon. When it vanished, the silence was as deep as the canyon.

"Follow me," said Skylar, pulling air into his lungs. He ran as far as he could, first with short, swift strides, then longer, lifting strides as each powerful stroke of his wings thrust him up, up, upward. Weedle pattered after him, with short, fast strides that never made it into long, lifting strides.

He rebounded off the canyon wall.

Skylar, who was halfway out of the canyon, made a sharp turn and almost nose-dived beside the discouraged Weedle.

Again and again they tried, but each time Weedle crashed into the stone cliffs and plopped down on the canyon floor.

"Skylar," whispered the exhausted, rumpled Weedle after the seventh attempt. In his next breath he meant to tell Skylar to fly out and away with the rest of the flock, but he could not muster the courage to say it. He was terrified to be left alone in the canyon.

The darkness had risen almost to the top of the canyon where the geese still looked down.

"One more time," said Skylar. He tried very hard to regain his glorious vision of the rescue and how it would go. "This time if you start to fall, I'll give you a boost." Then he saw it again: Weedle lifted on his back out of the darkness into the sunlight. His glistening wings. The triumph dance. Inspired by the vision of Skylar the Rescuer, Skylar charged, flapping his wings as hard as he could, forcing Weedle ahead of him until the two lifted off. Weedle was heading right for the canyon wall again.

"Higher! Higher!" shouted Skylar from behind him, and for an instant Weedle managed to gain altitude, but quickly faltered. With the agility of a hawk, Skylar dove underneath the smaller goose, then rammed him from below. This propelled Weedle a few feet higher in the air. The small goose hovered there, treading air like water, on the verge of another free fall. Skylar careened below him, his wings grazing the canyon walls as he flapped desperately to regain air balance. By the time he did, Weedle was dropping fast. Skylar could not save him now.

The geese and the Who-on watched the drama below with squawks and hoots and cheers and then *ooooh, nooo* as Weedle, after briefly rising, was sucked back into the shadows of the canyon. Then, miraculously, Weedle was back in the sunlight, somersaulting upward.

None of the geese realized it was the wind. The tricky canyon wind had returned with a blast, catching Weedle just before he hit the canyon floor and flipping him upward through the air. As suddenly as it had lifted him on its back, it dropped him again and vanished entirely. But Weedle, excited by his brief ascent and bolstered by the cheers of the geese above, found the will to flap his way the last few feet to the top of the canyon.

"I did it," shouted Weedle, still dazed from a headfirst landing at the feet of the others. "I did it!" he said, staggering in circles.

"You did it!" the geese trumpeted in unison, while Esther and Loomis did the triumph dance around Weedle. Roosevelt and the Who-on watched, both looking a little impatient. No one noticed Skylar. His air gymnastics had left him with barely enough strength in his wings to pull himself the last lap up and over the canyon wall. He collapsed, wings askew, in exhaustion at the edge of the cliff. It was not the triumphant return he had imagined for Skylar the Rescuer.

"Well," said Roosevelt after the triumph dance had dwindled to a few foot slaps and hoots, "if everyone is quite finished . . . perhaps we should fly in the *right* direction for a while."

Roosevelt strutted ahead to take the position of point goose, but Weedle rushed in ahead of him. "Let me, let me." He bounced excitedly, finding all his energy returned. "I can do it! I know the way!"

Roosevelt brushed the smaller goose aside. "You know the way, all right. The way into trouble," he snorted, and took to the air with more honking and flapping than was called for.

The other geese followed. This time the exhausted Skylar trailed, flying behind Weedle, just ahead of the Who-on. They flew due north once more, scanning the landscape for a safe place to roost, out of the way of the storm that seemed to track and taunt them. They settled in the same spruce forest where they had spent the night before and tucked themselves under the snowy boughs of a spruce. Now they were all together. The geese made little mewing sounds of connection before they buried their beaks in their shoulder feathers and slept.

CHAPTER 10
LOST POND

On the fifth day of their journey, the geese rose out of the shadow of the forest to meet the sun. The storm that had threatened slipped past, leaving only another dusting of snow. All thoughts of dangers were left behind them in the spruce forest. The flock sensed they were closing in on their destination, right down to Weedle, who asked over and over again, "We're almost there, aren't we? Aren't we? Skylar's done it! I'll bet it's just over that hill . . . isn't it?"

Skylar, at the point, flew straight ahead without answering. All the geese felt the nearness of the place and flew with strong, sure wing strokes.

None of the geese suspected that Skylar, looking so much like the point goose he claimed to be, was not at all sure where Lost Pond was in the succession of peaks and valleys and forests and ponds. The storm and the detour south to retrieve Weedle had confused things. He was no longer sure of the way. He wondered if Esther knew, but he dared not risk the humiliation of asking her. She followed close behind him without hesitation, as if she knew they were flying in the right direction. But what if she didn't know either? Panic staggered his flight. He had been following a picture in his mind of Lost Pond. Where had the picture come from?

The wild geese had said they followed the stars, the sun, the land, the rivers, but Skylar was not sure which of these he was following or if he was following them all at once. Now he wondered if he was following anything at all but his own overblown imagination.

Desperation overtook him. Skylar signaled for the flock to land. He circled above a small clearing on a mountaintop, turned against the wind to slow his descent, then spread his wings wide and glided downward. The other geese followed. They were tired but nonetheless surprised to land. They all felt very near their destination. Even the Who-on, who had come to expect almost anything from the geese, was unprepared when the geese suddenly broke formation and landed on the mountaintop. The Who-on perched in a hemlock and watched them with growing irritation, for the journey had already passed through four nights, and the time for the herons to begin their migration was getting close.

"The trouble with geese," muttered the Who-on to himself, "is they're always stopping to think things over."

"Why did we stop?" Roosevelt demanded once they had landed. "We must be almost there. My wings are strong and we had a good wind current."

"I could have flown forever," added Loomis with a swipe of his wings, which knocked Weedle over.

Weedle got to his feet and flung himself at Loomis, knocking him backwards a few feet, then Loomis, ever clumsy, lunged at Weedle, missed and sprawled on the ground. Then the two were rolling on the ground in full-blown battle while the other geese chattered back and forth about how far they'd come and how far they had to go to reach Lost Pond. The chattering and squabbling reached such a high pitch that a flock of cedar waxwings, feeding on pin cherries nearby, burst out of the trees in alarm. Still the squabbling rose higher and higher, louder and louder, as each goose tried to push its voice above the others. They were so busy making noise, they forgot to be cautious. The geese who had weathered storms, found their way out of caves and canyons, were not thinking of the dangers that lurked on land.

Just a few feet away, a coyote crouched beneath the flaming red leaves of a hobblebush at the edge of the woods. She lay so silent and flat, she was completely undetected by the arguing gaggle of geese.

The coyote's mouth opened slightly in a kind of smile and she began to pant soundlessly. She had never before come upon such fortune: geese landing almost in front of her, geese so plump and unsuspecting. Two of the geese were facing each other in a standoff just feet away. In one swift motion, she could have the potbellied one around his long, loopy neck and pulled under the hobblebush before the other geese knew what had happened. The coyote sucked in her breath, coiled her haunches and sprang. Just as she did, a violent storm of blue-gray feathers swooped down upon her.

The coyote leapt straight up, spun around and hit the ground running, yipping in terror as she fled. The commotion startled the geese and they scattered in every direction, honking hysterically, feathers flying, into the woods. Finally, only the Who-on remained standing on the mountaintop, wondering where the geese had gone and growing more impatient by the moment.

"The trouble with geese," he said very loudly, "is they talk too much."

"The trouble with geese," he continued, his long beak thrusting forward with each stride, "is they think things over too much."

"The trouble with geese," he said, spreading his wings, "is they spend more time down than up."

"The trouble with geese," he croaked at the top of his lungs, "is they have no sense of direction."

This brought Skylar waddling and huffing angrily out from under the hemlocks. "No sense of direction! How dare you? Who got you this far?" Hearing Skylar's voice, the others gained courage and poked their heads cautiously into the open.

"Yes," squeaked Weedle, still very shaken by the coyote attack, "who got you here?" Then Weedle looked around bewildered, silently asking himself the question that exploded from the Who-on:

"And where are we?"

The attention of the geese all swung to the Who-on. This was the first time they had seen the placid and unknowable bird angry.

"This does not look like Lost Pond to me."

It was also the first time they had heard so many words come out of him at one time. The geese all waited for Skylar's imperious reply. But he said nothing.

"It's just on the other side of the mountain," Weedle suggested, looking around at the geese.

"I'm sure it's not far now," offered Esther, a little weakly. Roosevelt and Loomis looked surly; the Who-on still looked angry, but Skylar offered nothing at all.

"Skylar. Tell the Who-on," Weedle urged.

"Yes. Tell the Who-on, Skylar. Where are we?" chided Roosevelt.

Skylar extended his neck as if he were finally about to answer, but not a sound came from him. He stared mutely past the Who-on and down at the geese. He could not tell them that he was lost, that the remembering light had failed him. There followed a long, expectant silence. Seldom are geese totally silent, and this silence seemed to grow wider by the minute, until it was wide as a lake with the Who-on and the other geese on one shore staring at Skylar on the other. Still, he could not bring himself to say the words "I am lost."

"What's that?" piped Weedle, stretching his neck in the direction of a peculiar sound that bubbled up out of the silence. They all turned to listen. Suddenly the hills erupted with a noise at once mocking and mournful. The geese recoiled. The Who-on was jubilant.

"We're there!" the big bird sang out, flapping his great wings and doing an odd, stiff-legged dance. The geese stared in amazement as the bird hopped from one foot to the other, then somersaulted in the air. The Who-on seemed to be on the verge of shaking himself to pieces.

"He's doing a heron's version of the goose triumph dance," whispered Esther.

Then, suddenly, the Who-on collected himself and took flight. The geese, not knowing what else to do, followed.

In a matter of seconds they came to a small marshland, circled by tamaracks still holding on to their golden needles and spruce at the bottom of the hill. Hunched dark forms draped the branches of one almost bare tamarack. A very strange convention, the geese thought. The birds roosting in the tree were now totally silent. The only noise came from the Who-on, who whooped and squawked as he hurried to join them.

The geese were used to seeing the Who-on as a singular bird, a perfect match for the trees and hills and ponds, but not for other animate things. Here the strange bird was no stranger at all. He dipped his long neck, took three hops and two wing flaps and melted into the mass of shrouded forms. The geese watched the odd convention from a corner of the pond. The herons did not seem to notice them.

"I thought the convention would be . . . more a convention," said Roosevelt, a little dismayed, "and Lost Pond—"

"More a pond," said Loomis.

The geese studied the dark mass of birds, the marsh, the surrounding trees. It was nothing like any of them had pictured.

"But this is it. This is Lost Pond!" exclaimed Esther.

"Of course," said Weedle, beaming toward Skylar.

Skylar did not offer any observations. He was too amazed that Lost Pond happened to be where it was. He glanced over at the little troop of geese and realized he was just as amazed by them. They were not the same geese of just four days ago. They looked tired, but at the same time, they looked strong and sure. Like real geese. Almost wild geese. There was less extraneous movement about them. Even Weedle, who was always hopping up and down, flapping his wings to get some goose attention, seemed to be more composed, at least for the moment, as he considered the convention of herons, his head lowered in concentration. Skylar moved closer to his flock. The geese turned to him expectantly.

"By my calculations, we flew ten thousand wing beats," he said. "Not counting the wing beats backwards, of course."

"Ten thousand wing beats," whistled Loomis. "Think of it." The geese passed this information among themselves, flavoring it with stories of caves and canyons, attacks from coyotes and raccoons, the appearance of deer and other geese, the triumph dance, the land beneath them, winds, the nights and sunrises. Ten thousand wing beats of adventure. This cheered the geese, who had begun to feel a little unwelcome at the heron convention.

"Of course," added Skylar, "if we were wild geese, we would be flying five hundred thousand wing beats or more." This statement settled the geese's feathers. They tried to imagine five hundred thousand wing beats of adventures.

"Five hundred thousand wing beats," repeated Roosevelt in disbelief. "That's not possible."

"But three days ago, ten thousand was not possible," said Esther. "And besides, it is not all flown in one day, but over many days."

"Esther, how do you know so much about it?" Loomis asked, for he really wanted to know how Esther, who had lived in the same pond for only a little longer than he, could have learned so much that he had not.

"Like Skylar, I was part of a migration once," replied Esther. Skylar jerked his head up. The other geese were surprised, too. They waited for Esther to continue, but it seemed she meant to say no more. She pulled her neck in close to her body and appeared to grow smaller and darker. Skylar knew she was fighting the old enemy, fear.

"My first migration ended in tragedy," she said finally, lifting herself above the fear the words brought with them. "A storm. Like the one we came through on the third day, only worse. My family and another family of geese were flying south for the winter. One minute there were bright skies for as far as we could see, and the next . . . there was a monstrous gray wall advancing on us. The other family of geese tried to fly over the storm, but they were torn out of the sky. My family tried to dive under the storm, but it caught us and scattered us to the earth like seeds."

"Into our pond?" asked Weedle.

"Onto a highway," she said, "far from that pond." There was another silence, quickly filled with an outburst from the herons on the other side of the marsh. "All of my family was killed, I think," she continued. "My wing was broken, but I was rescued by people. Then I was brought to the pond. I never flew again."

The other geese stared at Esther as if seeing her for the first time.

"I wanted to follow each time I heard the call of the geese, but even after my wing was mended, I could not find the courage to go. I answered their calls, and I waited for their calls back to me. That is how I kept my connection with the wild geese." She looked at each of the geese in turn.

"You understood the wild geese in the cornfield. They speak the same language. It just has more things in it, like where they've been, what they've seen, where to stop for the night, dangers along the way." She looked up at the sky. "The more places you go, the more language you learn. The more language you learn, the more places you remember. It's all there. You just have to listen."

The geese, even Skylar, who pretended not to be listening, struggled to understand Esther's words. They all followed her gaze to the sky.

"The more places you go, the more language you learn, the more language you . . ." Loomis halted.

". . . learn, the more places you remember," completed Weedle triumphantly.

"See!" shouted Esther. "You've got it. What one forgets the other remembers. That's what a flock is."

Now the geese were sure they did not understand, but Esther seemed so excited, they pretended to.

While the geese were pondering Esther's words and the ways of wild geese, Skylar was pondering the weird gathering in the tamarack. The closer he looked, the less sure he was about what he was seeing. He moved toward the tree, trying to understand the strange guttural language, the grunts and gurgles that passed among the birds.

Then as one of the birds in the group dropped to a lower branch, he saw clearly that whatever manner of birds these were, they were not herons. Skylar inched closer. They were huge, black birds, larger than geese or herons. He could now make out a twisted, hooked beak, a bald head and the most peculiar neck, half as long as a goose neck, drooping out of hunched shoulders. When they spread their wings, the creatures had a wingspan much greater than that of a goose or heron.

When one of the macabre birds turned to look at him, Skylar bolted upright in alarm, but his alarm call got stuck somewhere on the way. Wings spread, eyes bulged, beak opened and tongue wagged, but not a sound came.

Then one of the birds tore away from the others, spread its wings and lofted down from the tree. Skylar, still unable to utter a sound, stumbled backwards a few steps in terror. But the bird that landed in front of him was no stranger. It was the Who-on. He stood before Skylar, his usual stately self, head tilted to one side in just the way he always did to position the geese in his line of sight.

"No need to set off alarms," he said.

Hearing the Who-on's voice, seeing the Who-on standing before him, every bit the composed bird he had always been, Skylar closed his beak and settled his wings back at his sides.

"Those are not herons," he managed to say at last.

"No," replied the Who-on, his single golden eye settling on Skylar. "They are not. And this is not Lost Pond."

Skylar arched his neck at the Who-on as if unsure all over again what manner of bird he was.

"The convention, it seems, is over. It happened on the quarter moon."

Skylar continued to stare at the Who-on. Then he glanced back at the other geese, who chatted dreamily, unaware of this revelation.

"My memory isn't so good," said the heron. "I got the arrangements all wrong, it seems. You were right. I do have a very poor sense of direction. I lost it with my eye and my sense of time in the accident that landed me in your pond."

"Then who . . . what?" Skylar squinted toward the black, hulking forms in the tamarack.

"Turkey vultures," replied the heron brightly.

Skylar took a few steps backwards. He did not actually know many other forms of birdlife, and certainly he had never met a turkey vulture. But the habits of vultures, in general, he knew.

"Their ways take a little getting used to," said the heron, seeing Skylar's astonishment and obvious revulsion. "But they are one of us, after all. And they're going my way."

"You're migrating with turkey vultures?" asked Skylar, aghast.

"Thirty feet behind, of course," said the heron, with an exaggerated bow.

Skylar's attention was drawn once again to the bizarre birds in the tamarack. One of them shifted position in the tree, spreading its huge wings and revealing its decidedly unheronlike profile. Skylar stared in disbelief at the birds for a long time, seeing in them now nothing that could be mistaken for a heron. Then he turned his attention back to the Who-on.

"And . . . what about Lost Pond?"

"Still lost, I guess." The Who-on shrugged good-naturedly. "But only you and I know that," he added with a wink of his golden eye.

"Then what . . . body of water . . . is this?" Skylar's voice squeaked almost as high as Weedle's, finally drawing the attention of the other geese.

"Another to store in your memory. It won't stay in mine, I'm afraid."

At that moment, a terrible groan that raised the feathers all over Skylar's body emerged from the roosting birds, who seemed to fold and refold into themselves. The Who-on turned to look, then turned back to Skylar. "We will be leaving soon," he said. Then, with a thrust of his long neck, he took two hops and two wing flaps into the tree. After a few ghastly squawks and a brief adjustment of wings among the group in the tree, the Who-on was one with the turkey vultures.

"I wish you all a safe flight . . . wherever it takes you." The Who-on's last words issued out of the midst of the dark forms he was now a part of, just as he had become a part of everywhere he landed.

When Skylar finally turned to go back to the flock, they were all watching him with curiosity.

"The Who-on will be leaving soon," he said. There was not a trace of bewilderment left in his voice.

"Where will he go?" asked Weedle.

"To the big water," said Skylar without hesitation. The Who-on had said nothing about his destination, and Skylar did not know where the vision of the big water came from. His words had stepped out in front of him again, but this time, they had come not from the shallows of his vanity, but from someplace deep in his memory. He saw the big water as clearly as he saw the geese across from him. "They will fly through six more sunsets to reach their winter home at the edge of the big green waters."

The geese did not know where the big green waters were, but as Skylar spoke, an image flashed through their memories. It was a memory shared by all geese who fly the Atlantic flyway, one of the five migratory routes. However, for geese who had never called up this memory, it comes through in blasts of images.

"The big water," whispered Loomis, and he looked at Weedle to see if Weedle saw the same body of water in his memory.

"The Who-on said to tell you all that because of our *keen* sense of direction, he will now join his flock on the migration to their winter home."

"What else did he say?" asked Weedle eagerly.

"He said, 'I wish you all a safe flight . . . wherever it takes you.'"

"Wherever it takes you," repeated Weedle, giving weight to the Who-on's words. He turned to the other geese and saw the same excitement kindled in their eyes. "All the places we *can* go," he said, "now that we are *wild* geese." His voice slipped on *wild,* and the word twanged out of control against the hills. It was the last thing the geese heard before the darkness fell upon them. The word *wild* Weedle-screeched through their minds, settling there with a new knowledge. They had tested their wings and found their courage. They were wild geese now.

· · ·

Night filled the marsh, easing gradually to the top of the hills until only the sky was lit. The flock of geese found a hummock of sedges near one end of the marsh to spend the night. However, the woods were still too near and Skylar kept watch, spelled by Esther and Roosevelt.

As each of the three geese relieved one another at watch, they peered over at the edge of the marsh where the silent birds were crowded close together, almost indistinguishable from one another. The geese had the eerie feeling that the bulk of the birds had dissolved into the night.

Sometime later, when the waxing moon was almost overhead, the strange gathering of birds departed. It was as if the pond and trees and night itself had broken loose and risen into the sky with them. In the last light, the darkness became winged. In the pattern of wings that filled the sky, it was not possible to separate the turkey vultures from the heron. Once in the air, they were a beautiful sight, and all the geese fell silent watching their departure. Only when they were too far away to see did the flock of turkey vultures separate itself from the lone figure of the heron, who flew with steady, rhythmic wing beats, his head cocked on his back, legs against his body, thirty feet behind.

Then the birds and the light faded completely into the sky and the geese slipped their beaks under their shoulder feathers and slept.

CHAPTER 11
WILD GEESE

Just as the sun tipped its light into the pond, sending mists rising like night spirits, the flock of geese departed Lost Pond—or what all of the geese except Skylar thought was Lost Pond. Skylar flew at the point as strongly as ever, keeping to himself the knowledge that the herons were really turkey vultures and Lost Pond was still lost. It didn't matter now.

The geese broke into the sky, headed south. It was a solemn moment, but there was a sense of exuberance beneath the seriousness of the occasion. The geese knew, without speaking of it, that they would not return to their old life. This was a conviction they shared as a flock. They would fly beyond the man-made pond to the coast. They were wild geese now.

They announced their ascent to the surrounding mountains, as geese must. Into the bright air they rose, coming into sun as if out of the depths of water. With the approaching winter close behind, the geese flew with more urgency. Beneath their wings the air was a live thing, an element of their flight. The wind was theirs, just as it belonged to all winged, wild creatures. The geese sang out the joy of flight. It was a resonant, trumpeting song, except for Weedle's bark, which upset the harmony and gave this flock of geese a sound distinctive from other flocks that crossed the sky.

They flew all day, calling back and forth their reassurances and observations. Not a single argument arose. They flew with exhilaration, with certainty, with courage. As Skylar tired, Esther moved to the point, then Roosevelt. Weedle flew behind Loomis, at just the right height above and to the left of Loomis. Only occasionally did Weedle run up on Loomis's tail feathers, inviting a tumble through the air.

They flew on until they passed over the beaver dam pond where they had spent the night on the little island. Skylar remembered how he had wrestled with a fear that was far behind him now as he flew as the point goose of his own flock. They flew on, cleaving sky and distance. Beneath them the world had changed, even in the few days of their journey. The many colored lights that had been left on here and there throughout the woods were now turned off. The earth wore its timbered, before-the-snows plumage. The geese gathered all this in as they flew. Everything now was something to store in their memories. Each registered the fall and rise of the land beneath them, the trace of streams and rivers running to ponds and lakes, the patterns of trees, the stone fences, the fields.

While the geese were still strong on the wing, Skylar, at the point, cupped his wings and began a descent.

"Skylar," shouted Roosevelt from just over his wing, "we're good for another two thousand wing beats before nightfall."

"Perhaps," replied Skylar, "but surely you, Roosevelt, would not want to pass up a feast prepared for us." As the flock lowered, it appeared Skylar's keen eye had not failed. The land below was broken up into patchwork fields, each separated by thick hedgerows. The field Skylar's flock targeted for landing had been recently turned over. Bits of uprooted tubers and squashes were strewn across the surface. A few apples still clung like ornaments to the apple trees bordering the field, and the ground beneath the trees was covered with fallen apples, red as partridgeberries.

It looked as if the feast were prepared in honor of their migration. The geese descended upon the field in a clamor of excitement. They were eating before they folded their wings. They tore pumpkins apart, ate the seeds and pulp, gobbled down carrots almost whole. Their efficient beaks unearthed turnips and broken squashes. Through Skylar's mind flickered the warnings of the wild geese. He shot his head up now and then to scan the field, as he saw Esther doing, but was quickly drawn back to the feast.

The geese, riding the thrill of their successful journey to Lost Pond and their return to the wild, felt invincible, as if they had passed the test and could relax their guard. The world invited them to rest, to feed, to dream of where they would fly tomorrow. By nightfall, they were so heavy with feasting, they gathered together in one of the furrows in the middle of the field. From here, they were far enough from the surrounding woods to detect any dangers that might lurk there, but none of the geese took the role of sentinel that night.

He wondered, as his old pickup lurched over the ruts of the dirt road, what he was doing, anyway. The sun, barely risen, could only manage a bleak light through the leaden sky. An icy rain was sheeting over his windshield faster than the wipers could clear it. It was a Saturday morning. He should be in his warm bed. If only his words hadn't stepped out in front of him again at the mention of deer hunting. He'd even gotten permission from the farmer, who was happy to have a deer or two less to eat his corn next year. He'd gone so far as to offer the farmer some of the venison.

The farmer told him which field was the best to hunt, where the deer came each morning and evening to feed on the stubble of last season's corn. But bumping along the road in the dim light, he couldn't tell one field from the other. They stretched one into another, for miles it seemed, separated by hedgerows that still held solidly on to night. He could see his breath inside the truck. It

didn't matter which field, he decided. One was as good as another. He pulled over. Once he crossed this field, he would be in the woods. From there he would wait just out of sight of the field beyond. He tried to guess which way the wind was blowing but gave up. He started across the field, hopping over furrows until he reached the woods, which he quickly saw were even more impenetrable than they had looked from the road. Soon he was fighting through bramble and multiflora rose, fending off the thorns with the butt of his gun.

The woods descended into marshland, sheeted in thin ice, which he broke through and sank past his boots up to his knees. He cursed, wiped his nose on his sleeve, looked back the way he had come. The field he had crossed and the truck parked on the road could still be seen through the trees. He hadn't gone as far as he thought. It occurred to him then: How would he get a deer out of there if he shot one? Maybe he could ask the farmer to help. Where was the farmhouse from here, anyway? It was all getting too complicated. Maybe he could just find a rabbit to shoot.

He pulled himself out of the muck onto a tuft of cordgrass. Gradually, the ground rose up out of the marsh and it was easier to move, but he still couldn't see anything ahead but more and more of the same. He would go a little farther, he told himself, and if he didn't find the field soon, he would turn back. Then the touch of light ahead, the freshly turned black earth with the pinto pattern of snow upon it. He found a spot behind a moss-covered log where he was well hidden from view, but could still see the field clearly. He could almost see deer stepping into the field. His excitement began to rise.

But no deer. His wet feet and legs were growing painfully cold, and his fingers were numb. He set his rifle on the log and tucked his hands under his jacket. Fifteen more minutes and then he'd head back to the truck. He would stop at that diner he passed and have a leisurely breakfast. He'd be gone long enough to make it look good.

Then something moved. He didn't know what at first. Black, white. A wing tip? Geese? Slowly, he pulled one hand out from under his jacket and placed it on the rifle. Then the other. Could he hit a goose on the rise with a deer rifle? His fingers could hardly pull the trigger if he wanted to. But there they were.

. . .

Skylar awoke with alarm. He rose to his feet, neck outstretched. He scanned the field. Nothing moved. The other geese formed a little mound in the furrow, their feathers coated in a fine sheen of ice. He gave a sharp grunt and they came awake immediately, except for Loomis, who was always slow to awaken. Sensing Skylar's alarm, they shook the ice from their feathers and went quickly about the business of stretching their necks and legs and preparing their wings for flight. There was no squabbling this morning. In fact, there was little noise among the geese, except for a low guttural exchange. The message that something was wrong passed from Skylar to each of them. It wasn't just the slanting icy rain that said winter was now upon them. It was something else, some predator crouched just beyond the woods.

They gathered quickly in formation and without a single honk or a running start lifted themselves into the sky. Skylar, Roosevelt and Esther locked into formation, but Loomis, half asleep, faltered and couldn't gain height. Weedle ran up on his tail feathers.

"Higher!" ordered Weedle. "Or *I'll* be the fourth goose."

At this Loomis came awake. The blood surged into his muscles and he soared upward.

"You can be the Who-on from now on, Loomis," Weedle shouted from just over his shoulder. "I'll be—"

But Loomis couldn't hear the rest. At Weedle's goading, he shot up higher and clicked into formation right behind Roosevelt. He barely flinched at the crack of the gun. The flock was too high to worry about hunters anyway.

Skylar heard. He beat his wings harder, propelling the flock higher, faster than they had gone before. Something felt wrong. A piece missing.

"Weedle?" honked Loomis.

Skylar pulled up, hovered in the air. The formation broke apart, the geese treading air.

"Weedle?" Loomis called. There was no answer.

"Weedle!" they all honked over and over.

Skylar broke away, banked sharply and flew back the way they had come. The flock stalled in the air, then followed.

Flying against the wind and sleet, they could barely make out the terrain below, but they followed the blurry form of Skylar far ahead. Somehow he found the field among the quilt of fields below and hovered above it, trying to see through the icy rain and mist. Skylar dipped lower, pulled up. A man with a gun, leaning over something. A man with a gun stooping, prodding with the tip of his boot something in the furrow. Weedle?

Skylar flipped over and dove.

The man didn't see the huge goose until it had swooped past, almost knocking him over. Frightened, he raised his gun and shot at the goose over and over. But before he could get a good aim, the goose was flying around him in circles, honking so loudly he could hardly tell which direction it was coming from. He shot in all directions, off balance, terrified by the rocketing bird that pummeled him with its wings and blare of honks and hisses. He grabbed his kill by the neck and ran for the woods.

Skylar flew back and forth over the woods where the man had disappeared, honking the contact call to Weedle, but Weedle, who had followed him everywhere, did not answer.

The rest of his flock, traumatized and exhausted, gradually lost height until they were within rifle range themselves. It was time to make a decision. Time to leave Weedle behind. This time, for good.

Gathering his strength and senses, Skylar honked a contact call to the geese and flew up to meet them, then they tilted their wings south. They flew as high and as fast as they could.

The geese flew until they were many miles away, until the sound of gunshots had silenced, flying by the pull of the way, but too frightened to land. It was only when they could go no farther that Skylar guided them into a pond in the middle of a field. From here they could see the approach of predators. A thin skin of ice had settled over the shoreline as they plowed through it and into the deeper, ice-free water at the center of the pond. Skylar, who now balanced the danger of ice with other dangers, judged by the air temperature the pond would not freeze that night.

The geese were dark forms bobbing in front of him on the disturbed surface of the pond. They were silent and wooden as decoys riding the turbulence they had created until the fear of guns quieted one by one inside them.

For a long time, the geese did not speak. Then, finally, Roosevelt said in a stunned voice, "Weedle is dead."

A small, pained gasp rose from one of the geese.

"He was killed by a hunter," Roosevelt continued. "Hunters kill geese. If we had been in our own pond, no one would have shot Weedle." Roosevelt did not say this to blame, but because it was true. "As long as we are on the wing, we can be shot, too."

A tremor of terror ran through the geese. Nervously, they scanned the fields surrounding them. The wide-open spaces no longer seemed to beckon them. They were a trap.

"We must go back to our pond," said Roosevelt finally. The geese turned to him, but none answered. Even Loomis, once Roosevelt's echo, could not repeat these words. Loomis and each of the wild geese tried to call up the memory of the pond they had come from. The memory was very far away, though they knew the pond itself was only a day's flight. Soon they would fly over the pond or return to it. Soon they would enter the world beyond or end their journey where it had begun—to fill their days waiting and watching and wondering where the wild geese flew. Soon they would choose. They looked to Skylar.

Skylar bobbed in the water opposite them, a dark, silent form. They could not see how he looked back at them. They could not see the grief and despair he felt for ignoring the lessons the wild geese tried to teach him. He thought of Weedle, a clump of feathers in the furrow of the field, and he could not utter a word. It was Esther who finally spoke.

"We cannot decide now," she said in a voice staggering with grief. "Tragedy still hovers over us with its terrible wings." She looked to the skies as if seeing it there. "We must wait until it flies away. Then we will know."

CHAPTER 12
THE LAST OF THE FALL MIGRATIONS

The geese slept fitfully that night on the shore of the pond. Many times, one of the geese would straighten its neck and peer into the moon-bright night, then gradually recompose itself back into troubled sleep. Just before morning, Skylar awoke to a familiar sound. Out of habit, he looked for Weedle. But Weedle was not there. Disoriented, Skylar gazed at the world around him.

Everything had changed in only a few hours. A frost had settled, covering the rushes that grew beside the pond and the feathers of the geese with a glittering shawl of light. The pond itself glowed like a lantern under the full bloom of the moon. Skylar was so amazed by the scene he remained transfixed, staring at the geese as they unfolded, one by one, from their enchanted slumber. As they came awake, each goose immediately looked to the skies. They heard the sound, too. It was the call of wild geese, coming from very high, from very far away, a sound as magical as the world that glittered around them.

"Did you hear that?" said Skylar breathlessly, only now fully awakening to what came to him on the call from the distance.

"It's Weedle," shouted Esther in amazement. "I'd know that call anywhere."

"Weedle?" Roosevelt snorted. "How can it be Weedle? Do you forget what you saw with your own eyes?"

But Esther, the sky watcher, kept her eyes trained on the horizon as if she were sure Weedle was there.

The call came again, but fainter, one odd note jutting above the others. This time each of the geese, even Roosevelt, responded with their distance contact call. The night rang with the call of geese ricocheting across the distance.

"We must go," said Esther excitedly. The geese stirred in indecision, looking from one to the other, and finally all of them to Skylar.

"Weedle . . . is dead," said Skylar slowly. "We saw with our eyes." The geese lowered their necks to the ground. "But inside of us he lives," Skylar continued. "What one forgets the other remembers." The geese raised their heads, their necks like flagpoles. "We cannot forget what we are. We are *wild* geese now." He said the word *wild* just as Weedle had said it, zinging off into the distance.

The call came again, fainter still, but this time Skylar's flock rose to it, honking at the top of their lungs in response, spraying frost from their wings, rising into the sky.

They followed the geese, which were now very far away, tracking them with the distance call that stretched between them as faint as the ribbon of morning that opened in the east. They flew on and on. Shortly after noon, they passed over the pond where they had lived, empty of geese, and began their longest journey.

The woman heard the *ker-honk,* yelp, bark of the geese before they broke into view.

"They're coming." She jumped up, upsetting her cup, spilling tea across the crossword puzzle she had been working on and scattering the birds at the feeder outside the kitchen window.

"They're coming?" she asked the cat crouched under the kitchen table and eyeing her warily.

It had been almost a full week since she and her great-granddaughter had counted what they thought was the last of the geese. She fumbled for her glasses, then her binoculars, then without waiting to find her boots, she rushed out the door in her socks. There was no time to climb to the top of the hill. The geese were already in sight. From where she stood, just feet outside the doorway, it appeared the geese barely cleared the crest of the hill.

She counted each silhouette as it crossed the sky through the bare branches of the maple. A flock of twenty-four geese passed. Then one, two, three, four, closely behind. Stragglers, she guessed. She would add these to the notebook, revising the year-end count of geese. One hundred and eighty-one, she could tell her great-granddaughter.

The icy wind that came from the north with the geese told her they had left just in time. These would be the last wild geese to count this year. The last of the fall migrations.